Perfect Stranger.

The first novel in

the Perfect series.

Written by

Lindsey Powell.

Except for the original material written by the author, all mention of films, television shows and songs, song titles, and lyrics mentioned in the novel, Perfect Stranger, are the property of the songwriters and copyright holders.

To all my friends who needed a bit of Jake in their life!

Chapter One.

This is it. This is how I am going to die. I would never have imagined my life ending in this way. The fear coursing through my entire body only moments ago, has now been replaced by a feeling of shock. My body trembles as I acknowledge an agonising pain in my left side. Everything is becoming hazy, making it difficult for me to register exactly what is happening to me. Time seems to stop as I try to focus on my surroundings. Unfortunately, I can't seem to divert my focus from the immense pain that is spreading through me like wildfire. My head throbs from where it smashed against the floor when I fell only seconds ago. I dazedly manage to lift my head slightly so that I can look to my left side, where the pain is all consuming. It's difficult lifting my head up off of the floor as all I want to do is give in to the darkness that beckons to me. It takes all of my remaining energy to move, and when I look down, I see shiny metal sticking into my side. My mouth starts to fill with saliva, and I desperately swallow it down, willing myself not to vomit. The red substance seeps out of my side and is starting to saturate my clothes. My blood. Lots of my blood. I try to call out, but my mouth doesn't want to cooperate. I let my head fall back to the floor and my eyes begin to feel heavy. I fight the urge to close them, but the darkness seems so inviting. Images flash through my mind rapidly. So many images and memories, and so little time in which to process them all. In the distance, I can hear some sort of commotion. An evil laugh brings back the element of fear, and then there's the sound of footsteps beside me. I hear a voice shout, 'NOOOOOOOOOOO,' which alerts me to who's voice it is.

The voice shouting brings me comfort. Such a beautiful voice. I let go of the fear and let my eyes flutter shut. A pair of arms feel like they are enveloping me. Strong arms that hold me in their embrace. It brings a warmth, that I wasn't expecting, to this moment. I try to open my eyes once more to look at what I know will be the most beautiful face I have ever seen, but all of my energy has left me. I stop fighting the urge to sleep, and I let the darkness slowly seep in. The images return and flicker through my mind, until they stop at one particular moment of my past.

Full lips grazed my cheek softly as he leant in to whisper,

"spend the night with me." A statement, not a question.

His words made my insides melt. My knees felt

like they were going to buckle beneath me. Excitement raced

through my core. Butterflies fluttered wildly in my stomach.

His heated breath on my skin was enticing. He smelt incredible. His

voice deep with smooth undertones, luring me to accompany him.

Sparks jolted through my body as his hand found a resting place at the bottom of my back. A delicious tingling ran through me and

arousal radiated from my body.

The memory fades and the image of caramel coloured eyes fill my brain. The eyes of my perfect stranger. The mere sight leaves me gasping for my final few breaths. Through the fogginess, I am abruptly pulled back to reality for a few seconds by three simple words.

"I love you." That beautiful and comforting voice is lulling me into a secure feeling. With the images and memories now gone, those final words imprint on my last waking moment. I finally give in. Darkness has consumed me.

Chapter Two.

Three weeks earlier.

"STACEY! What the bloody hell is taking you so long?" Charles bellows up the stairs, his voice making me cringe.

"I'm coming. Will you keep your voice down!" I shout back to Charles.

"Well for goodness sake, get a move on. We need to leave in the next five minutes." I can hear the irritation in his voice. He is such an impatient man. How I ever thought that I was in love with him, I will never know. Charles is my boyfriend. We have been together for nearly three years. I used to think that I was quite lucky to have caught his eye. His short blonde hair and dark green eyes were what first attracted me to him. I am a sucker for nice eyes. His athletic body wasn't bad to look at either. Don't get me wrong, he wasn't what you would call ripped, but he certainly wasn't lacking in the abs department. To be fair, Charles still has a good physique as he likes to take care of himself. When we first started dating, he was kind and charming. He would take me out for dinner and to the movies, and we had a fairly decent sex life. Not outstanding, but satisfying enough. He seemed to want to look after me, and I craved that feeling. It was a feeling I had craved ever since my Nan had passed away. My Nan was my rock, and she looked after me from a young age. I was nine years old when my parents were taken from me. They died in a horrific car crash. A little piece of me died along with my parents on that day. The two most precious people in my life were taken in such a brutal way. The crash wasn't even their fault. It was caused by some drunk driver, who obviously couldn't resist the urge to drive rather than walk. My Nan instantly became my legal guardian. She embraced her role and made me feel loved and cared for. I worshipped her. She took me on, an angry little nine-year-old girl, and made me into the woman I am today. Well, the woman I was before Charles came along. I think that, if she were around today, then she would be disappointed by my life choices at this moment in time. I try not to think about that too much though. My Nan died three and a half years ago, after a long battle with cancer. I was devastated. There isn't a day that goes by that I don't miss her, and of course my parents. I was twenty-five when my Nan died. She never met Charles. I don't know what she would have thought about him. Charles came into my life six months after my Nan's death. I am not close to many people, so at a time when I was vulnerable, Charles managed to get through to me. My best friend, Lydia, has never liked him. She says that she has had his card marked since the day I introduced her to him. I never let her dislike of him phase me though. He wanted to care for me and that was all I wanted at the time. How ridiculously naïve of me. I should have listened to Lydia.

"STACEY! COME ON!" Charles bellows again, breaking me from my thoughts. I roll my eyes, quickly finish applying my lip gloss and take one last look at myself in the full-length mirror. I am wearing the most gorgeous red, floor length, lace dress with killer red stiletto heels. The fabric of the dress hugs my body in all the right places, and gives me just the right amount of cleavage due to the slight plunge from the neckline. I look classy, and of course the dress has been pre-approved by Charles. He is such a control freak. I have my long brunette hair loosely curled and swept to one side, where I have placed a clip so that it flows down my right shoulder. I have kept my make up to simple nude shades as I don't want to distract from the dress. I have small silver hooped earrings in, and a plain silver bracelet on my left wrist. The bracelet has sentimental value as my Nan gave it to me for my twenty-first birthday. Pleased with my appearance, I quickly make my way down the stairs, to find Charles waiting by the front door with his car keys in his hand, tapping his foot and glaring in my direction. "Finally! Why do you always insist on making us late for everything?"

"We're not late. If I was to come down the stairs looking slightly dishevelled then you would moan that I embarrass you, and we can't have your colleagues seeing us as less than perfect now, can we?" the sarcasm drips from each word that I speak. Whilst muttering under his breath, Charles passes me my coat and ushers me out of the front door and towards his car. His brand new, flashy, range rover sport that he purchased this morning. We couldn't possibly be seen in my car, the boring bog standard ford fiesta. Heaven forbid that people see us arriving in any vehicle that's isn't classed as 'posh' by Charles' standards. Once in the car we sit in silence, and my mind starts to wander. How did things become so bad between us? How have we lost the respect that we used to have for one another? Maybe he has never respected me, and it is only since living together that I have noticed? I took the plunge and moved in with him six months ago.

Charles had been pestering me for a few months, prior to me giving in, about living with him. He made me an offer I couldn't refuse and I agreed to share his home. The offer was one in which I would be able to become a full-time writer. My dream is to become a published author, and Charles used this reason to finally get me to say yes. He told me that I could give up work and that he would look after me. Now, up until that point, I had never been a kept woman, but I am so passionate about my writing that I had to seriously consider his proposal. At the time, I was working at The Den and I had been there for five years. The Den is a club/bar that is thee place to go on any night of the week. It was where I first met Lydia. I loved my bar job, but it was never my lifelong dream. I took a few days to think about what Charles had offered, and I came to the conclusion that if I was ever going to devote my time to becoming a full-time writer, then this was my chance. I told Charles that I would move in with him, and he seemed delighted, leading me to think that I had made the right choice. How wrong could I have been? Very as it turns out. I handed in my notice at The Den and moved in with Charles a few days later. Within two weeks of moving in with him, Charles started to show his true colours. Granted, I had seen some of his bad traits on occasion, but doesn't everyone have bad points? Maybe I was just too ignorant to see those traits executed to their full extent beforehand? He was only ever badly behaved when in relation to his business, and even that wasn't very often. His bad behaviour had never been directed at me. If I ever questioned him about the way he was acting, then he would always have a perfectly good reason as to why he acted in this manner. Me wanting to be loved and cared for, I fell for his excuses every time. I saw Charles as the closest thing to family that I had. What an idiot I truly was! The first week of living with him was good. In fact, it was so good that I was kicking myself for not moving in when he has asked me the first time. He made me dinner every night, bought me flowers and generally made me feel special. I bragged to Lydia about how great he was being, and generally made her feel sick with my renewed affection for him. I should have kept my mouth shut, because week two brought with it the real Charles Montpellior. He became an absolute nightmare, and he still is to this day. I remember it clearly, the day it all changed. It was a Monday evening and the start of my second week of living with Charles. I was quietly sat in the lounge, watching the evening soaps on the television, when Charles walked in with a folder tucked under his arm. I didn't take much notice as he brought work home with him all the time. He is the owner of J & M Accounting. On this Monday evening however, Charles picked up the television remote and turned the television off. I looked at him, appalled that I was unable to watch the rest of my programme. He sat down, in the chair opposite me, and I was about to ask him what he was doing, but the look on his face stopped me. His serious expression had me sitting up to attention.

'Now that you have been here for a week, I feel I need to set some ground rules,' he said. *Ground rules?* I must have looked confused because he quickly carried on talking. 'I have a list of things here that I would like you to adhere to. I feel it is only fair, seeing as you no longer work.' His expression was so serious that I almost wanted to laugh. I didn't though. His comment about me not working stung a little. I wanted to argue back that it was his idea for me to stop working, but he continued with his little speech. 'In this folder, you will find lists of what I find acceptable. If you could read this tonight, then from tomorrow, you can start to follow these routines and rules.' It wasn't a question; it was an order. Charles placed the folder on the coffee table between us and then stood up. 'I will be in my study if you need to discuss anything.' With that, Charles strode out of the room. I looked at the folder as if it were going to bite me. What on earth does he mean by routines? I sighed, picked up the folder and opened it to the first page. There were ten pages in total, each one detailing what he expected of me. There was a cleaning rota, a shopping list, a weekly allowance budget for myself, and a schedule of when I would be required to attend functions with Charles. I honestly thought that he must have been playing some sort of joke at first. I said as much to him, only to be greeted with a scowl. It was the following morning, and onwards, that I realised that I had made a mistake. I had just turned twenty-eight and here I was being instructed on how to live my life. I managed to follow the routines and lists for the first few weeks, and then I thought I would mix it up a bit. I don't mean drastically, I just mean that instead of cooking lasagne on the Wednesday, I decided to cook it on the Monday. This did not go down well with Charles, and resulted in him having a complete hissy fit at me. I can only compare his tantrum to that of a two-year-old toddler. It was ridiculous for a grown man to be acting this way. I recall the poisonous words he spoke to me. You would have thought that I had threatened to castrate him with the way he went on. Charles then sulked about the lasagne incident, or lasagne-gate as I call it, for the next week. Yes, a whole fucking week! I told Lydia, and my friend Martin, about his behaviour and neither of them were surprised. In fact, I had to stop Lydia from marching round to our house and giving him what for. She's extremely feisty and protective of her friends. Martin on the other hand has to be careful, seeing as he works for Charles as an event planner. Martin has been a witness to many of Charles' outbursts. He's also been on the receiving end of a few of them too. Martin has worked for Charles for the last three years. We got chatting at an event two years ago, and we have maintained a friendship ever since. A secret friendship that is, as Charles would never approve of me befriending his staff. Martin has such an infectious personality. I adore him. It is hard to meet up with him though, as every time I go out, I am asked numerous questions by Charles about where I have been and who I have been with. After six months, I suppose I have got used to the interrogating. So, here I am playing the dutiful girlfriend, and making sure that others think Charles and I have the perfect life. Hell, I have gotten so good at putting on a show that I could probably pursue a career in acting! Whilst I have perfected my outer shell, on the inside I am in turmoil. I am bored. Bored of being his arm candy, bored of having my life planned out for me, and bored of having no chemistry whatsoever, sexually or otherwise. I'm sure no one could really blame me for losing my sexual appetite though. We have sex once a month, on a designated night of Charles' choice. Although, we have given that a miss for the last two months, much to my relief. I crave the feeling of intimacy and love. I fantasise about having the types of orgasms and sexual trysts that you read about in romance novels, or that you see in the movies. I love to read and often have my nose in a book. However, it is not just the story that grips me, it is also the escape a good book gives me. It's like a time out from my real life. I can almost imagine that I am the heroine in a novel, and that I am the one who is being seduced by the man that worships her on a daily basis. My mind often wanders back to the only one night stand that I have ever had. It was the night before I moved in with Charles, and my last shift working at The Den. I know I shouldn't have done it, but this guy was so mesmerising. That night was one of the best nights of my life. God, how pathetic does that sound? I didn't even ask his name, I just knew that I needed to be with him and give my body to him. And by god did he take it. Even now my body hums at the mere memory of him.

"And for god sakes, don't say or do anything stupid. Last time you made a fool of yourself as well as a fool of me." Charles, once again, interrupts my thoughts. His voice holds nothing but anger and disgust.

"Charles, I didn't do anything wrong." I sigh, bored. We must have had this conversation about a hundred times. He is like a broken record.

"Oh please, your dancing was atrocious. I had to excuse your behaviour for weeks afterwards." He actually screws his face up as he speaks.

"If I am such an embarrassment to you, then why the hell are you taking me to this event?" I ask, exasperated. Anyone would think that I had done a bloody strip tease for the entire room with the way he goes on about it.

"People will expect you to be there. It will look bad if you don't accompany me. I don't need people asking me questions about where else you might be. I don't have time to make excuses for you." Charles leaves no room for any more discussion on this topic. I can't be bothered to respond anyway. I am deflated. I feel beaten down by him. The situation I am in is beyond dire. The truth is that Charles has merely become a means to an end for me, and has been for a while now. If I leave Charles, then I won't be able to continue being a full-time writer. Selfish, I know, but this is what it comes down to. I should have kept a few of my shifts at The Den, but no, I stupidly thought that he might just want to see me succeed in my writing career. I now see that he just wanted me to become his personal skivvy. He always hated me working at The Den. Charles maintains that he hated all of the male attention that I received, and before I moved in with him, I genuinely believed that was the reason. Now however, I realise that Charles wanted me at his beck and call. It was also not a 'posh' enough job for his girlfriend to have. I mean, in Charles' mind, the thought of saying that he lived with a bar maid must have been so beneath him. I miss my independence. I suppose he thinks he can treat me how he wants now that he controls all of my finances. Three years of my life have been dedicated to this relationship, obviously not taking into account my one night of dalliance. I think it took moving in with Charles to see that we really aren't a good match. I like to take each day as it comes and enjoy life, but Charles is incapable of that. I personally think his bad traits all come from his mother. Oh my, he is a mummy's boy in every sense. I really don't like his mother, and the feeling is mutual. Charles is an only child, born into a rich family. His mother, Margaret, always lets him have his own way. Charles and his mother share the worst trait of all, being a snob. Margaret has always been very vocal about how Charles deserves to be with someone better than me. These types of comments used to hurt me, but I just ignore them now. Over time I guess you just learn to grow a thicker skin to hateful words. His father, James, was the complete opposite. He was such a lovely man. He died two years ago from cancer. Bloody cancer seems to take all the good people away from me. Either that or a car crash. James dying is how Charles acquired fifty percent ownership of J & M Accounting. The company is known in various countries around the world. Charles does work hard to make sure that the company is running to a high standard, but would it kill him to take one day off? Apparently so, according to him. We haven't had one whole day together, by ourselves, for over a year. When I had my own job, and I didn't live with him, I suppose we managed to make time for one another. Something we stopped doing and took for granted, or at least Charles did anyway. Charles' money is far too important to him nowadays to pay any attention to his girlfriend, also known as the live-in maid! I seriously need to rethink what I am doing. I don't know how much longer I can put up with his behaviour. I never pictured myself being with a man like this. I am nearly at my breaking point.

The drive to the Bowden Hall takes about twenty minutes, and that is where tonight's event will be held. We regularly attend functions here, and its beauty never ceases to amaze me. The vast grounds are spectacular, with luscious green grass that is always maintained to the highest standard. It never looks like anyone has set foot on it. The gardens go on for miles, with beautiful flowers lining the driveway, all the way up to the stunning building that is the Bowden Hall. The building has big sash windows and eighty rooms in total, which are all decorated with the finest antiques and painted in the richest colours. Golds, reds and greens are the main colours throughout. It makes you feel like you have entered a building out of a fairy tale. We pull up to the front doors and the valet comes straight over, standing to attention by the car, waiting for us to get out so that he can go and park it at the rear of the building. Charles gets out, not bothering to walk around and open my door for me. I emerge from the car and walk around to take my place by Charles' side. I know the drill.

"Now darling, make sure that you smile and generally adore me," Charles says, smirking. God, you would think that he was fifty odd instead of being twenty-nine years old with the way that he talks. I could quite happily slap him, but instead I plaster a fake smile on my face as we walk up the steps and enter the building. The entrance hall is vast, with an impressive cascading staircase leading to the first floor. The butler, stood by the door, greets us politely as we walk past him. To the left of us is the Great Ballroom, which is the room that tonight's event is taking place in. There are four other rooms on the ground floor, but Charles always insists on using the Great Ballroom for events. I presume it is because it is the biggest and most lavish room of them all. As we enter, I admire once again how stunning the décor is. From the gold-plated trim to the crystal chandeliers that hang above us. The lighting of the room is soft and intimate, ready for the dinner and dance that is about to begin. I take a flute of champagne from a passing waiters tray.

"That's right, on the booze already," Charles snarls in my ear.

"Oh shut up Charles. It's a party. There are drinks all around. Now lighten up," I say sweetly, keeping the smile plastered on my face as I speak. I can see that he wants to retaliate, but Martin is walking over to us, so Charles kisses my cheek instead. Keeping up appearances is in full swing.

"Ah Martin," Charles says. "Wonderful party so far, eh?" Ugh, I think I am going to throw up. What an idiot.

"Oh yes. It has been a pleasure planning this event sir," Martin responds, ever the dutiful employee. Martin then turns to me and takes my hand. "Looking as beautiful as ever Miss Stacey." He places a kiss on the back of my hand which makes me smile. Martin does a good job of acting like we are just acquaintances at these events. I give him my most dazzling grin. His partner, Clayton, is also just as charming. They make a wonderful couple. Martin has toned down his look for this evenings event. Normally he would be wearing some sort of fluorescent coloured clothing, but tonight he dons a simple black tuxedo and white shirt combo. His black hair is swept to one side and gelled to within an inch of its life. His blue eyes sparkle and his goatee has been neatly trimmed. He looks very handsome and nowhere near his thirty years.

"Why thank you Martin. You don't scrub up too badly yourself," I say to him. Martin chuckles and excuses himself to go and promote his party planning skills to the other guests. Can't say I blame him for wanting to get away from Charles as soon as he can. Seeing him at work five days a week is bad enough, but having to pander to him on a Saturday night must be torture.

"I wish you wouldn't talk like that to my employees. You sound so common," says Charles. I feel anger course through my body. I cannot listen to this man for a moment longer.

"Well, I hope this is common enough for you; fuck off Charles." With that, I turn on my heel and leave him to go and find someone more interesting to talk to. Although, that is a challenge in itself seeing as nearly everyone here is probably just as stuck up as Charles is. I can feel my blood boiling at how much of a dick Charles is being. I walk through the throngs of people, smiling politely and saying the odd hello here and there. As I approach the back of the ballroom, my eyes rest on a gentleman with his back to me. I stop walking and admire his stance, which even from the back, is commanding. For some reason, my body begins to react to him. There is a humming radiating through me, and the hairs, on my body, stand to attention.

Goosebumps cover my entire being and I shiver as the man starts to turn around. I feel the breath leave my lungs and butterflies make an appearance, in my stomach, as his eyes lock with mine. His caramel coloured eyes, so beautiful that I could get lost in them. His silky, jet black hair is styled to perfection, and his lips look so soft and kissable. The slight stubble on his chin gives him a handsome rugged look. I can't believe that I am looking at him. I squeeze my eyes shut. I must be dreaming. But, when I open my eyes, he is still there. He is standing a few feet away from me, looking like a God. This can't be happening. My sex clenches with excitement as I continue to look into his eyes. Time stops. I never thought I would ever see him again. My one-night stand. My perfect stranger.

Chapter Three.

I stand on the spot for what feels like hours, but in reality, must only be a few seconds. I cannot move. My feet feel like they are glued to the floor. My mouth has gone completely dry. He is talking to someone else but his eyes never leave mine. His gorgeous, penetrating eyes. It has been six months since I had my wild night with this man. I truly thought that I would never see him again, but here he is, in the flesh, at my pompous boyfriend's event. I have never seen him at any events that Charles has thrown before. I feel someone pulling on my arm and I feel the sudden urge to swat them away like I would an annoying fly buzzing around me. I blink a few times and manage to avert my eyes from my handsome stranger, only to come face to face with Margaret. I can't help but roll my eyes. Of all the people in this room who may want to speak to me, it has to be her. She looks angry and I know that I am about to face her acidic tongue.

"What do you think you are doing young lady? How dare you walk off from my son like that. You are making yourself look ridiculous and not to mention childish. You are lucky to be classed as his girlfriend Stacey. Now go back and treat him with the respect that he deserves!" she hisses each and every word at me like a ticked off snake. Her pudgy face is screwed up in distaste. I guess a simple hello wouldn't have sufficed. The years have not been kind to Margaret Montpellior. Her hair is completely grey and is pulled back into a tight bun. There are multiple crow's feet around her eyes, and her double chin wobbles as she shakes her head at me. Margaret is only a short woman, but she doesn't shy away from anyone who pisses her, or her son, off. Her nose is wrinkled at me in disgust, and I feel something shift inside me. I can no longer bite my tongue.

"Excuse me Marge," she hates it when I call her that, "I really don't appreciate being spoken to like that. After all, you wouldn't want me to make a scene now, would you?" The look of shock and disbelief on her face is priceless. I can't deal with her right now. "I am not going to stand here and argue with you. Just tell Charles that I am going to get some fresh air, and when I am ready, I will be back to carry on our sham of a relationship." I don't wait for her to respond. I turn and walk towards the entrance hall. I can't believe I spoke to her like that. I can normally keep a lid on my emotions, but something has happened to my brain to mouth function. The look on her face is one that I will forever keep logged in my memory. I feel a smirk creep across my face, and I do nothing to try and hide it. Seeing my stranger has thrown me. I quickly make my way through the guests who are still entering the ballroom. I head out to the front gardens and keep my head down to avoid eye contact with anyone. I am not in the mood to make idle chit chat right now. I walk into the first garden and find a secluded area behind one of the glorious rose bushes. The scent that radiates from the flowers is heavenly. I sit on a dainty little white bench, which looks onto a pond that is filled with koi carp fish. No one can see me sat here behind the rose bush. I sit and watch the fish happily swimming about. What with Charles, Margaret, and my stranger all in the same room, my brain is in overload. I close my eyes and let out a sigh and am instantly frozen in place when I hear, "surely it's not that bad to run into me?" Oh my god, that voice, so smooth. It's him! My stranger! Shit! I seem to have lost the ability to speak. I take in a deep breath and open my eyes. I turn my body in the direction of his voice and I raise my head so I can look at his eyes.

"I didn't think I was so scary that you had to run off," he says whilst suppressing a smirk. My gaze settles on his mouth and my tongue darts out to moisten my dry lips. My mind is screaming at me, *get your shit together Stacey!* Oh god, what do I do? My body reacts to him in much the same way as it did when I saw him in the ballroom. The humming is racing through me, and I have to clench my sex as it starts to stir. He is just watching me, waiting for me to respond. I clear my throat and manage to get my voice to work.

"Well, not scary as such, but maybe a bit underdressed for the occasion," I say with a hint of sarcasm in my tone. Of course he doesn't look the slightest bit underdressed, but it was the first thing I could think of to say. I am totally out of my depth. I need to remain calm and not allow myself to panic.

"I don't think I did too badly," he says, holding his arms out either side of him so I can get a look at his full form. Even with his tuxedo on, I can see his body is well cared for. Hell, I can remember his body being like a work of art. He slowly turns around and my eyes fixate on his pert behind. My, my, my, he really is breath taking. It's a good job that I am sitting down, otherwise I think my knees would have given way by now. His black tuxedo is complete with bow tie and he looks good enough to eat. Looking very smart in his ensemble, he manages to ooze a cool yet casual vibe.

"Judging by the look on your face, I would say you agree," he says, still smirking. Shit, now I just look pathetic and am probably a few seconds away from having drool running down my chin. I am struggling to form words, which is something I have never really struggled with before. *Think Stacey, think!*

"Okay, so you do look very handsome in your tuxedo, but then so do the other men in this place." *Oh yeah, great move Stace. Making yourself sound like a tart who eyes up other men is the way to go with this. Genius. You should have just kept your mouth shut.*

"Have a wandering eye do we Miss..."

"Paris. Stacey Paris." I hold my hand out for him to shake, praying silently that he doesn't notice that I am quivering. He steps closer and takes hold of my hand. I feel sparks shoot through my body as our skin connects. My eyes go wide as I stare into his caramel pools. He lifts my hand, bends down, and places a kiss on the back of it. I draw in a long, shaky breath and squeeze my legs together. *How can he have this effect on me? I barely know the guy.* I clear my throat. "And you are?" I enquire.

"Jake Waters."

"Jake Waters," I repeat. I know that name. *Why do I know that name?* I cast my mind back to a conversation I overheard Charles having a few weeks ago, and it suddenly dawns on me. "Jake Waters? As in Jake Waters who owns the company Waters Industries?"

"The very same," he replies. *Fuck!* I didn't realise that was who he is. Well, why would I when all I did was fall for his charms in a bar and spend the night with him in a moment of madness, without even asking his name. He frowns at me. "Why do you look like you have just seen a ghost?" I realise that he is still holding my hand. I abruptly pull my hand away and jump up off the bench.

"Uh, I have to go. It was nice to meet you, *again*," I say, as I dash past him and head back to the entrance of the Bowden Hall. I walk as quickly as my stilettos will allow me to. He looked taken aback by my reply, but I can't let myself get into a proper conversation with him. My heart beat is pounding and I feel dizzy with the realisation of who I have slept with. Charles will flip his lid if he ever finds out. Jake Waters owns one of the largest companies in the world, and it ranges in all types of business, from accountants to construction. The guy is a multi-millionaire and he's only thirty-three years old. Jake also happens to be the rival accountant company for Charles' firm. Oh, and Charles just happens to hate Jake's guts. I try to calm my breathing and stop myself from shaking. The last thing I need is Charles noticing my current state and asking me a hundred and one questions. I stand outside the Great Ballroom and take long, deep breaths. When I have managed to regain some composure, I enter the ballroom. The guests are all sat down and are being served their starters. I scan the room, looking for Charles, and spot him at a table right in the middle. I steadily walk towards him, although he seems to be far too engrossed in conversation to notice where I am.

"I'm sorry that I took so long," I say to Charles as I take my seat beside him. "I just needed to clear my head." Charles looks at me for a few seconds and then returns to his conversation with another guest at the table. He doesn't even speak to me. I am mortified. How dare he make me feel so worthless. I quickly look at the other guests sat around the table and hope that none of them just witnessed Charles humiliating me. Most of the diners are immersed in their own discussions but Martin, who is sat opposite me, is looking directly at me. I give him a weak smile which he returns with a frown. I just shake my head at him and avert my gaze. I quietly start to pick at my duck starter. I would much rather be eating a burger to be honest. All this rich, posh food makes me feel a bit sick. Putting my fork down, I feel goose-bumps cascade over my body as I see Jake walk across the room and sit at the table next to me. He is staring at me and I can almost feel his eyes undressing me. The hot pool gathering between my legs would suggest that I like the thought of him undressing me. Shit, I need to get a hold on my body's reactions to him. I watch as Jake picks up his glass and raises it in my direction. I quickly look away. So, not only have I got my feelings to contend with, but now Jake will be able to see that I am here with Charles. The last thing I want is to become a pawn between the two of them. For all I know, Jake may decide to hold me to ransom over the fact that we slept together. I'm really hoping that Jake keeps his mouth shut about what happened between us. I dread to think how Charles, and his precious mother, would react if they were ever to learn the truth.

Chapter Four.

Charles acts like an ignorant ass throughout the entire meal. I also have to endure Margaret staring daggers at me the whole time, with her beady little eyes. On top of that, I have to keep my eyes from wandering over to where Jake is sat. This really does go down as the most uncomfortable event that I have ever attended. Once the dessert has been cleared away, we are all asked to move to one end of the room so that the staff can quickly clear the tables away for the dancing part of the evening to begin. I am relieved that the meal is over. As I stand, Charles grabs hold of my hand and leads me to a corner of the room.

"Why did you speak to Mummy the way you did earlier?" He is not happy one little bit. It makes me cringe that he calls her Mummy. I roll my eyes as I sense a storm brewing, and I don't mean the mother nature kind. God, Charles and his Mum are like a tag team; piss one of them off and the other one comes at you too. I don't stand a chance against the both of them.

"She was going on at me and I snapped. I came here to support you, but all I seem to get is grief, and to be quite honest, I'm bloody sick of it," I say quietly. As much as I would love to embarrass Charles in front of all these people, I really don't need them knowing that my love life is a sham.

"Well, have a little more respect next time," he hisses at me. I smile at him through gritted teeth and turn away. I spot Jake leaning against the wall just along from us. He is talking to Martin. I wish I could go over there and just be near him, but I know that I can't. I turn back towards Charles and dutifully stay by his side whilst the ballroom is prepared. After about fifteen minutes, the ballroom is ready and the band are all set up to play. The band start off by playing some jazz music which has a great vibe. I feel my body start to sway in time to the music.

"Do you want to dance Charles?" I ask him, even though I know that he will say no.

"No thanks. There are people that I need to speak to." With that he walks off and starts chatting to some young blonde woman. I don't feel remotely jealous. I do however feel rejected. I know that we're not in a great place, and haven't been for some time, but a little attention wouldn't go amiss. I could cry through sheer frustration at my situation. My head is all over the place.

"I'll dance with you." I look to the side of me to see that Jake is still leant against the wall, but somehow, without me noticing, he has managed to sneak right up next to me.

"I don't think that's a good idea," I tell him.

"Come on, one dance won't hurt. I promise I'll let you lead," he smirks. I feel a smile creep across my lips. Why the hell shouldn't I dance with him? My boyfriend certainly isn't interested in doing so. "You have a beautiful smile." I can feel the blush on my cheeks from Jake's compliment. Thank goodness the lighting is dim in here. I give into the temptation and grab Jake's hand, pulling him onto the dancefloor. The band finishes playing their jazz number and start to play James Bay, Hold Back The River. I love this song, but maybe dancing to this isn't the best idea, what with it being a much slower pace. I am about to make an excuse when Jake takes both my hands and places them on his shoulders. He then puts both of his hands on my hips, causing my adrenaline to sky rocket. I am frozen in time and butterflies start doing somersaults in my stomach. I am aware of everything he is doing. Nothing and no one else exists in this moment as we start to dance to the music. He leads and I follow, and we dance in silence for the first half of the song. Jake is staring into my eyes, which makes this moment seem significant, for reasons I can't comprehend. I know that if Charles can see me, he will be furious, but I really don't care. I will deal with the fallout later.

"So, Stacey," Jakes says, breaking the silence between us. "Why did you run off from me?"

"Oh, I knew that the food was being served at any moment, so I thought it best that I get back," I reply. Jake chuckles quietly and leans towards me, putting his lips right by my ear.

"I don't mean tonight Stacey. I meant when we had our first encounter together all those months ago." Oh god! I feel my heartbeat quicken and my sex start to stir. I am positive that I look the colour of a beetroot right now. I am a little shocked that he even remembered me. Then again, I never forgot him. I'm not quite sure what to tell him, so I simply stick to the truth.

"We met in a bar, we went back to yours and had sex. Then, when the morning came, I left. That's how it works isn't it?" I manage to make myself sound cheap from my brutal description. It was so much more than sex, but how am I meant to say that to him? I am doing a fantastic job of impressing people tonight!

"I suppose it is. I wouldn't know though. It's not something that I would usually do." Jake says with a wink.

"Me either!" I say a little too loudly. A couple dancing near us looks over and I manage to smile politely at them. I feel my defences rise at Jake's comment. He probably thinks that I am just some floozy who will jump into bed with anyone. I can hardly blame him for thinking that I suppose, but I am still going to put him right on the matter. "That was the one and only time that I have been crazy enough to go home with a stranger and have a one-night stand. Don't think that I make a habit of it buddy."

"Whoa, calm down. I didn't mean it to sound like that. I just wondered why you left whilst I was asleep. I didn't mean anything by it, I promise." Jake stares into my eyes and I know that he is telling me the absolute truth. Why do I feel like this around him?

"Ok. Sorry," I say, my anger slowly ebbing away. I should really think before I react sometimes. I suppose I am just so used to Charles putting me down that I expect every guy to do the same thing. "I didn't think that you would want me there the morning after, so I left. It was only meant to be a one-night thing. I have a boyfriend," I say coyly.

"Ah, you mean the ever charming Charles Montpellior." Jake's voice is laced with sarcasm.

"Uh, yeah. I guess you figured that out huh?" *Now you just sound fucking stupid Stacey. Of course he figured it out.*

"Yeah," Jake laughs. "Were you guys together when you slept with me?" I avert my eyes from Jake in shame at his question. I can't bear to admit that I cheated on Charles. "I'll take that as a yes."

"I know it looks bad. I know what I did was terrible, but I just needed to clear some stuff in my head, and I needed to be wild, just once." I try to explain my scandalous behaviour. "I never intended to come back to yours, it just happened."

"So coming back to mine was a mistake then?"

"God no!" *Oh god Stace, tone it down and make yourself sound less eager.* "I meant to say that you were not a mistake, but I just needed one night out of my reality. One night where I did something for me. Just one night where I did something wild and enjoyed it." Jake is smiling and I am now aware that we are slow dancing to a completely different pace of song. We must look ridiculous.

"So I was your wild something?" Jake asks.

"Yeah. You could say that. Sort of like my perfect stranger." *Oh Christ, did I really just say that out loud? I need to stop embarrassing myself and get the hell out of here.* I break away from Jake and stand a few feet back

~ 33 ~

from him. I feel flustered and need to regain my composure, which I am not going to achieve by being near him. Jake puts his hands in his trouser pockets and I ache for the loss of contact. "Thanks for the dance Jake, but I really need to go and find Charles now." With that, I walk off of the dancefloor and go in search of Charles. I can feel Jake's eyes on me, burning into my back as I walk away.

Chapter Five.

I find Charles sat at the bar with the same young blonde woman that he was talking to earlier. He doesn't appear to be aware of Jake and I dancing together just now. Thank goodness for that. I roll my eyes at the sight of the woman hanging on his every word, and I go and interrupt their conversation. I stand just behind Charles and tap him on the shoulder.

"I don't mean to interrupt, but I would like to go home now please." Charles turns around and scowls at me.

"What? We can't possibly leave yet darling. We need to mingle some more. Would you like a drink?" Charles looks, and sounds, utterly pissed off that I have intruded on him talking to this blonde woman. Whoever she is, she sits there with her legs crossed in front of her, and the slit of her dress reveals the top of her thigh. Her make-up appears to have been applied with a trowel, and her breasts look like they are trying to make a bid for freedom from her low cut dress. Christ, it barely covers her nipples! She is twiddling a lock of her long blonde hair around her finger. An obvious sign that she is flirting with Charles. She smiles at me, but I can sense that she would rather I just disappear. This woman clearly doesn't care that I am Charles' girlfriend. I sigh and turn my attention back to Charles.

"I don't want a drink. I want to go home," I say a little more forcefully.

"We're not going anywhere yet so just stop being so rude." Charles then turns away from me and continues his conversation with the blonde. That's it. That is the final straw. I have had it with him. I whirl around on my heels and march towards the entrance hall. I ask the butler if he would kindly call me a taxi. He says that he will and he goes off to fulfil my request. I am so mad at Charles right now. He has done nothing but humiliate me and make me look stupid all evening. I can feel my blood pressure rising and I can't wait to get out of this place and put tonight behind me. I stand by the front doors and tap my foot impatiently as I wait for the butler to confirm he has ordered me a taxi. Whilst I am waiting, I can sense Jake approaching me. I look in his direction as he exits the Great Ballroom. Oh god, he is so handsome. His eyes are fixed on me as he comes closer. He reaches me and runs his eyes up and down my body, making me feel as if I am stood naked before him. I feel a blush creep up my neck and reach my cheeks.

"Going somewhere?" he asks me.

"Not that it is any of your business but yes, I am going home. I am just waiting for my taxi to arrive." My tone comes across as rude. I don't mean it to be, but I also don't want him to see the effect that he has on me. Plus, I'm still really pissed at the way Charles has treated me tonight.

"Uh, Miss?" the butler interrupts us, diverting my attention from Jake. "Your taxi will be here in the next fifteen minutes."

"Thank you," I politely answer. The butler nods his head and goes to resume his position, stood opposite Jake and I, by the front doors.

"I can give you a lift if you like?" Jake says, seemingly unaffected by my rudeness towards him only seconds ago. It takes me a moment to control my shock at his suggestion.

"Um, that's really not necessary."

"Look, I know it will be difficult to keep your hand off of me, but surely it beats waiting around for a taxi?" Jake says, trying to make a joke of it. I feel a slight grin start to tug at my lips at his playful nature. I would love him to give me a lift, but it's dangerous territory, isn't it? I think back to how Charles has treated me this evening and decide that I should live a little.

"Oh go on then," I say, not taking more than a few seconds to make up my mind. His mouth breaks into a grin and he holds his arm out to me. I link my arm through his and, as we walk out of the Bowden Hall, I apologise to the butler and tell him that I will no longer be needing the taxi he has ordered for me. If the butler is annoyed, he doesn't show it. He just simply nods his head and bids us goodnight. Jake leads me to a sleek black limo waiting out the front.

"This is yours?" I ask him, astonished. Jake laughs and signals for the driver to wait in the car.

"It sure is." Jake opens the door and gestures for me to get in. The look on my face must say it all. I thought that Charles had plenty of money, but Jake is clearly in a different league. Charles has never had a limo escort us anywhere. The thought is actually quite surprising, seeing as Charles is obsessed with flaunting his wealth. I enter the limo and sit back into one of the glorious leather seats. It is so soft. My ass literally sinks into the seat. I hope it doesn't leave a massive dent when I get up!

"So, where is it we are going to Stacey?" Jake asks as he enters the limo and sits opposite me. I am very conscious of the fact that our legs are inches apart. The thought of brushing my leg against him is enough to make me want to jump his bones. I shake my head and try to concentrate on calming my nerves, which are rapidly becoming overwhelming. What was I thinking? Getting into a limo with Jake was not a good move. The images of our one-night stand come flooding back to me. His mouth, his touch, his body, his...... "Stacey?" Jake's brow is furrowed as he gives me a questioning look. Shit, I must have zoned out for too long. I clear my throat, which has gone dry. I manage to relay my address to him and there is a distinct quiver in my voice. The thought of returning home isn't exactly filling me with pleasure right now. Going home, and later being confronted by Charles, fills me with dread.

"I don't know about you, but all that fancy food doesn't exactly do it for me. Want to grab a burger and fries on the way to yours?" Jake asks as he hands me a glass of champagne that he has just poured. Champagne in a limo is not how I thought I would be escorted home tonight. I take the glass off of him and gratefully take a sip, enjoying the bubbles making their way down my throat.

"Now that sounds like a brilliant idea. You really are perfect aren't you?" And there I go again. My brain really needs to engage with my mouth before I speak. I take a few more gulps of the champagne, hoping that the alcohol will enable me to speak to Jake without making myself sound like a complete fool. Although, I am pretty sure it is having the opposite effect. Jake laughs and instructs the driver, through an intercom in the side of the door, to go to the nearest burger place. We travel in silence as I continue to drink my champagne until the glass is empty. I feel Jake's eyes on me the whole time, but I keep my gaze averted. If I look into his eyes, then I know that I am going to say or do something stupid. Feeling awkward, I am glad when we reach the burger place. I go to get out of the limo but Jake stops me. He asks me what I want and then he exits the car, leaving me alone. I look around and realise that the driver must still be sat in the front. I am way out of my comfort zone here. For all I know, Jake could be a complete psychopath. For some reason though, I just know that he isn't. I eye the champagne bottle, which is by the side of Jake's seat, and I quickly pour myself another glass. I am just finishing off the last drop when the limo door opens and Jake climbs in, burger bags in hand.

"Voila. Cheeseburger and fries madam," Jake says in a French accent. I stifle a giggle.

"Why thank you kind sir." I smile and Jake gestures for me to eat my food. I unwrap the burger and try to be as lady like as I can whilst eating it, but is it really possible? Burgers are one of the messiest foods to eat in front of a man. Especially a man that is a virtual stranger but is someone who makes your stomach do somersaults every time he looks at you. I decide to just take small bites. This will stop me from getting burger sauce all around my mouth anyway. Jake finishes his food whilst I have barely eaten half of mine. I should have just ordered some fries and left it at that. My appetite wains as Jake speaks to the driver through the intercom.

"Hey Eric, do you mind just driving around for a while please?"

"No problem," I hear Eric say.

"Why are we driving around for a bit?" I ask Jake as I take another miniscule bite of my burger and then put it back into the bag it arrived in.

"I want to get to know you a little better before you leave me again." Jake's eyes almost burn with intensity. I try to remain calm and just focus on keeping this conversation casual.

"Oh." I feel breathless. What could he possibly want to know about me? Only one way to find out. "Okay, what do you want to know?" I have managed to make myself sound normal, and by normal I mean that there is no wobble in my voice betraying how nervous I am. *Excellent Stacey, nice and relaxed.* I give myself a mental clap.

"I want to know what I have to do to get another night with you?" Jake says, his voice low. His eyes have a wicked glint in them, and all of a sudden, I feel like I am his prey. Oh shit, calm and relaxed has deserted me.

"Excuse me?" I say, breathlessly. The wobble in my voice is back. I was not prepared for a question like that. What ever happened to simple questions like, what's your favourite colour?

"You heard me Stacey. I remember everything that happened the night we slept together. You are not a woman that is easily forgot." I gasp at his honesty, and I can feel that I am losing myself in those beautiful caramel eyes of his. My panties are becoming wet with my need for this man. Time seems to stop as Jake's hand touches my thigh, making my whole body vibrate. As his fingers gently stroke the top of my thigh, I close my eyes as I try to wrestle with my emotions. My body is screaming at me to give in to my urges, but my head is trying to make me realise what my actions could result in. I am torn. Seeing as I have made no attempt to stop Jake, his hands continue their exploration of my body. He slowly trails his hands up either side of my ribcage, stopping when he reaches beside my breasts. I let out a soft sigh. I can feel his breath getting closer to my face.

"Look at me Stacey." I slowly open my eyes and stare at his facial features. He has just the right amount of stubble to make him look even more desirable than he is already. His skin is flawless and lightly tanned. I know that if he kisses me, then I won't be able to stop myself from giving in to him. His lips are millimetres away from mine.

All it would take is for me to lean forward slightly for our lips to connect. As I battle with myself about whether to kiss him or not, Jake smirks slightly, and then moves his lips to my neck. I place my hands on his chest, feeling his hard body beneath my palms. He showers my neck with light kisses before tracing along my jaw line with his tongue. It feels so good. My hands travel down from his chest, and I am just about to untuck his shirt so that I can run my hands over his body, when my phone starts to ring, jolting me out of our embrace.

"Fuck," I say, a lot louder than I intended to. I quickly push Jake off of me and grab my clutch-bag. I find my phone and see that it is Charles ringing me. I am not even tempted to answer it. I let the call go to voicemail. I think it is safe to say that reality has just imploded on whatever planet I thought that I was on only seconds ago. "Jake, I really need to be getting home now."

"Are you sure?" Jake asks. He is sat opposite me again, with his arms resting on his knees so that he is leaning forwards. He looks at me with a slight frown and his head tilted to one side. I feel as though he is trying to reach into my soul.

"Yes I'm sure. I'm going to be in enough trouble tonight without adding anything else to the list." I can't look at him as I speak. Jake doesn't argue with me. Out of the corner of my eye I see him push the button on the intercom. He instructs Eric that our drive is over and that we need to go to my address. I straighten out my dress and just stare out of the window for the journey home. I must look like a complete slut, what with the one-night stand and now this limo scenario. I mentally kick myself for getting into this type of situation. Jake doesn't attempt to speak to me, which I am grateful for. I fear that if he did, I would just make a fool of myself. It only takes ten minutes to reach my house. I ask Jake to pull up a couple of doors away so that Charles doesn't see me arrive home in a limo.

"Thank you for the food and the ride home Jake," I say, still refusing to look at him.

"No problem. It wasn't quite the ride I had in mind, but there is always next time." My head snaps up to look at him and our gazes lock. I must look dumbfounded as I try to find words, but nothing to say comes to my mind. Instead, I pick up my bag, quickly exit the limo and briskly walk to my front door. *What did he mean next time? There can be no next time!* The limo doesn't drive past my house until I am walking in my front door. I shut the door and slump against it, trying to regain my composure. I have had to try and regain that a lot tonight! I almost expected Charles to be waiting by the door, tapping his foot, but it turns out that he isn't even home yet. Once I feel like I can walk without my legs giving way, I make my way upstairs to the bedroom. I carefully take off my dress and get into my comfy pyjama bottoms and vest top. I then take off my make-up, and tie my hair into a ponytail, before climbing into bed. I would rather be asleep before Charles gets home. At least that way, the argument we are most definitely going to have can be postponed until tomorrow morning. I glance at my phone and see that Charles actually left me a voicemail when he phoned me, whilst I was with Jake. I reluctantly listen to the message, only to find out that he isn't coming home tonight. He's staying at Mummy dearests for the night. Relief surges through me. I place my phone on the bedside table and close my eyes. I can feel the smile pulling at my lips as I imagine the things Mr Jake Waters would have done to me in that limo before I succumb to sleep.

Chapter Six.

I don't wake up until ten o clock the following morning. I am normally an early riser, but I must have needed the sleep. I slowly get out of bed and go to take a shower. I let the warm water cascade over me as I pleasure myself following last night's events with Jake. I have so much pent up sexual frustration that it is the only thing I can do right now to help relieve some of it. Images of Jake running through my mind means that it doesn't take me long to reach my climax. Even in my mind, Jake manages to make me feel things I have never felt before. Once satisfied, I get out of the shower, dry myself and throw on some skinny jeans and a white vest top. I don't bother with any make-up. It's not like I am going to see anyone that is worth putting it on for. Lydia has always told me that I don't need make-up. She says that I am a natural beauty. In fact, she is more complimentary of my looks than my boyfriend is. I grimace at the thought of facing Charles at some point today. He hasn't returned home yet and I am dreading the tantrum that he is bound to have the minute he walks through the door. I push any thoughts of him to the back of my mind and pick up my laptop. It is a glorious sunny day outside and I decide to walk to the local coffee shop for my morning caffeine hit. I will attempt to do some more writing to escape the thoughts of my current reality. I put on my white sandals and grab my handbag on the way out of the front door. It is only a short walk from my house to the coffee shop. I love being able to do things like this without having to worry about work. I am very lucky to be able to do such things, but that luck comes at a high price; being with Charles. The coffee shop, called Danish, that I go to is a regular haunt of mine. When I enter, I see that Bonnie is working today. She is a lovely girl, still at college and very happy go lucky. She has a petite frame and the longest dark brown hair that I have ever seen. It literally goes below her butt and that's when it is tied up. God knows how long it is when it's down loose. She sees me walk in and instantly signals for me to sit down and says she will bring over my usual order of black coffee and a fresh croissant. I smile at her and sit at my favourite table, in the corner, right next to the window. There are only a few other customers in here at the moment so it's nice and quiet. I put my laptop on the table and settle down in my seat. Time to get myself into writing mode. Bonnie comes over, once I have set my laptop up, and places my food and drink by the side of it.

"Hey Stace," she greets me. "How was the party last night?" I happened to be in here the other day and I mentioned to Bonnie that I was going to a function last night. I suppose function automatically translates as a party in her eyes.

"Ugh, not great." I can feel my face pull into a grimace.

"Oh dear, that bad huh?"

"Afraid so. I'm going to need several cups of coffee to keep me writing this morning."

"Well, I'm here until three this afternoon, so I'll make sure that your cup is filled if I see that it's empty."

"Thanks Bonnie," I gratefully smile at her as she bounces off to deal with another customer. I stare at the few pages that I have written in the last few weeks, as I eat my croissant. So far, I have written half of the book, but if I want to leave Charles and get my life in order, then I really need to get a move on and finish it. I may think that the writing is the hard part, but once I am finished, I have the job of obtaining a publishing deal. I am hoping that it won't take long to do that, but it is a tough market out there. I have read countless interviews of famous authors who were rejected more than a few times before being given their big break. I try not to dwell too much on this though. I need to believe in myself and hope that an agent or publisher will see something special in my novel. Before I know it, I have devoured my croissant like it is going out of fashion. I am about to start typing when I sense someone standing in front of my table. I look up and am shocked to see that it is Charles.

"Oh. Hi," I say, thrown by his appearance.

"Hi."

"What are you doing here?" I try not to sound too annoyed at his arrival but I don't think I manage it.

"When I got home and saw that you weren't there, I figured you would either be here or at Lydia's place. Lucky for me it's not the latter." I don't fail to notice the sarcasm in his tone at the mention of Lydia. His feelings for Lydia are the same as hers are for him. They hate each other. "So, I thought I would grab a coffee and, if you were here, then I would see what you were up to. I feel bad that we didn't get to spend much time together last night. Give me a sec and then we can catch up. Would you like another coffee?" Well, this is new. He has never come here before to spend time with me. I politely decline his offer of coffee and watch him as he goes to order his. He's wearing black khaki shorts, a loose white t-shirt and sandals. His hair is damp so I presume that he hasn't long got out of the shower. I watch him and feel empty. No emotions are present. He returns moments later and I shut my laptop lid as I just stare at him with a puzzled expression on my face. He sits opposite me, looks at me and sighs.

"Stacey, I'm sorry for the way I treated you last night. It was wrong of me to ignore you. I should have been a better boyfriend. Please accept my apology?" My eyes are wide and my mouth has dropped open. I must look shell shocked. I open and close my mouth, like a fish, for a few seconds before I can find any words to reply to him.

"Okay," I say, slowly as I feel my eyes narrowing with suspicion. "What's up Charles? Something is wrong for you to come and find me and apologise. Don't get me wrong, it's very nice to hear an apology, but it's just not the norm. Help me out here because I'm a little confused." I can see he is struggling to respond, but I need to know what has gotten into him. I lean back in my chair and fold my arms across my chest, waiting for him to answer.

"I just feel that I should treat you a bit better, that's all." He has a guilty look on his face. Charles doesn't do guilt, so this is a whole new experience for me.

"And that's it? You just feel that you should treat me better?" I am not convinced in the slightest that this is the reason he has come to find me, and he knows it. I see his breathing begin to quicken and he looks so uncomfortable that it is making me uncomfortable. He starts to squirm in his seat.

"Stacey, you know that I love you, don't you?" He looks into my eyes and I realise that I'm not sure I care enough to hear what he has to say. Maybe I need to make more of effort too? I don't fail to notice that his declaration of love does nothing for me. There's not even a spark of emotion igniting within. This is also the first declaration of love that I have had from him in months. My suspicions are heightening by the minute. I need to see where he is going with this.

"Okay Charles. If that is all that is really bothering you, then we can go home and talk things out." I decide to play along for now. I will eventually find out what the real issue is here. Charles will crack under my interrogation; I am sure of it.

"I would like that. As long as I don't distract you from your writing. Why don't you come home in a couple of hours and I can cook us a nice lunch, and we can talk then?" Wow, he is really pulling out all the stops.

"Okay. Sounds good." I force a smile on my face as he leans over and kisses me on the cheek. He then leaves the coffee shop. I still feel perplexed by the way he is acting. I sit with my third cup of coffee, and go over the conversation Charles and I just had. Whilst he was here, I noticed some signs that he was nervous, but due to my shock I guess I didn't process them at the time. But, now I replay it, he was very fidgety and perspiring ever so slightly. Something is wrong. This doesn't feel right, and it doesn't sit well with me. *Shit, what if he chucks me out? I will have nowhere to live and no income. Oh my god, that has to be it. He's being nice to throw me off the scent. There is no way it can be anything else.* I quickly shut down my laptop and leave the money, for what I have consumed, on the table before saying a rushed goodbye to Bonnie. I need to go and speak to Lydia. Maybe she can help me figure out what Charles is up to. After gathering up my things, I walk to the front door, only to collide with someone.

"Shit," I say as I feel my laptop slip from my grasp. Lucky for me, the person that I have collided with manages to catch my laptop before it hits the ground. I let out a sigh of relief and divert my gaze away from the laptop. Oh god, of all the people I could have bumped into, it had to be Jake. My heart does a little flutter and I stare at him, flabbergasted. *What the hell is he doing here?* I seem to have lost the ability to speak and I just stare at him like some lust filled teenager. I try to calm the hormones that are raging through my body. I suddenly feel very self-conscious of my plain appearance.

"In a rush Miss Paris?" Jake's smooth tones make my knees weak.

"Uh, yeah," I say, breathlessly. *Pull yourself together woman, he's just a guy. An extremely hot guy that you happen to be attracted to, but still just a guy none*

~ 50 ~

the less. "Sorry, I didn't mean to bump into you. I guess I should pay more attention in future." I avert my gaze from his as I struggle to get my breathing under control.

"Well I have to say, of all the people who could have bumped into me, I am pleased that it was you." *Oh Christ, does he have to be so charming?* I giggle like a school girl. "So, I guess you don't have time to get a cup of coffee with me?" Jake looks at me with those smouldering eyes and all I want to do is give in and spend some time in his presence, but my brain decides to wake up and reminds me that I have to go and see Lydia.

"I'm afraid not. I need to be somewhere. Maybe another time?" I instantly regret the words as I say them. Another time? What am I thinking? I can't be within five feet of the guy without my brain going into meltdown.

"Shame. But I will hold you to that 'other time' Miss Paris." Jake flashes his megawatt smile at me. It takes all of my willpower not to change my mind.

"Nice to see you Jake," I say as I step around him and start to walk away.

"You too," I hear Jake say behind me. I resist the urge to turn around, but I know that he is watching me. I can feel it in every fibre of my being. It isn't until I get around the corner that I let out the breath that I have been holding.

Chapter Seven.

I rush to Lydia's flat, which is about a five-minute walk away from Danish. It's good that she lives so close. I fly up the stairs, knock on her door and wait for her to answer. I tap my foot impatiently whilst I wait. Lydia answers the door a minute later looking like she has had a very good night indeed, judging by the sight of her. Her long, auburn hair is all in disarray and her clothes look like they have just been thrown on her body in a hurry. I can't fail to notice the great big grin across her face and the twinkle in her emerald green eyes. I'm guessing her boyfriend, Donnie, has given her a night to remember. *Ugh, Donnie.* He makes my skin crawl, but he seems to make Lydia happy, so I keep my opinions to myself. The last thing I want to do is fall out with Lydia over my feelings of her choice of boyfriend.

"Hey babes," she says, cheerfully. "Come on in and make me a coffee. You can have one yourself if you like." Yep, typical Lydia. That's why I love her so much. She's so welcoming and full of life. We have been best friends for the last five years. We met at The Den. She is the one who hired me. She is still running the place now, which hardly surprises me, as she is great at her job. I go through to her little kitchen, put my laptop and handbag down, and click the kettle on. I presume Lydia went back to her bedroom as there is no sign of her. I shout out, "I presume Donnie wants a cup as well?"

"Yes please Stace," Donnie's voice says, making me jump. My back was to the doorway of the kitchen, and I didn't hear him approach. I turn and see that he is leant against the door frame, wearing only a pair of jogging bottoms, which are hung loosely on his hips.

"Christ, you scared the shit out of me! Go and make yourself guest appropriate would you?!" He just laughs at me and ignores my request as per usual. Donnie has no qualms about letting visitors see him in half of his clothes. Actually, if it was up to him he would probably walk around naked, but I think Lydia puts a stop to that when there is company present.

"You mean you want me to hide my body and deprive you of the privilege of seeing this?" Donnie says, as he points towards his body. I roll my eyes and try not to be sick as I make the drinks. I hand Donnie his mug and he saunters away like a slithering snake. I shudder and pick up mine and Lydia's drinks. I make my way through to the lounge to wait for Lydia. I'm surprised Lydia can put up with Donnie's massive ego. Donnie doesn't come back and join me in the lounge, which is a relief. However, just in case he changes his mind and comes in, I choose to sit in the armchair rather than on the sofa. That way he won't be able to sit by me. He may look relatively good with his olive skin, shaved head, brown eyes and muscly physique, but he really is a slime ball and Lydia just can't see it. He must be fucking awesome in bed for her to stay with him. Lydia waltzes in a few minutes later looking a little less dishevelled.

"Good night then, huh?" I ask her.

"Fucking fabulous babes," she says as she takes her seat opposite me on the sofa and picks up her cup of coffee. "So, what's up?"

"Why would anything be up?"

"Because you look a little pale and I can just sense these things you know. Call it best friends intuition." Damn her. She's right. She always knows when something is wrong with me. I sigh and fill her in on what happened with Charles last night and this morning.

"Oh dear, that doesn't sound too good. Very out of character for him isn't it? Or maybe he really has just realised that he's got a good thing with you? It may have taken him three years to finally see this, but hey, miracles do happen," Lydia ponders sarcastically. I raise one eyebrow at her and she rolls her eyes. "Don't look at me like that missy. He treats you like shit and you know it." I sigh at her but she continues to speak. "Look, I know I'm not his biggest fan but come on babes, you are gorgeous and have a great personality to match. He would be a fool to lose you."

"I don't know Lyd. I think something has happened and he's going to chuck me out of the house. Maybe it's because I snapped at his mother at the event last night. Or maybe it's because he actually did see me dancing with Jake, or maybe…….." I am cut off abruptly by Lydia.

"Whoa, whoa, whoa. Wait just a minute. Who is Jake?"

"Oh, um, you remember the guy I went home with from The Den, the night before I moved in with Charles?"

"Oh good grief, how could I ever forget him! What a gorgeous hunk of man he was!"

"Yeah, him, that's Jake." I then proceed to fill her in on what happened at the Bowden Hall and about what happened afterwards in the limo. I relay all of the information to her quickly so that she can't interrupt me whilst I am in full flow.

"Well, that's just fan-fucking-tastic Stace!" she screeches at me when I have finished. "But, I don't understand why you pushed Jake off of you?" Her reaction is what I was expecting. Lydia does not believe that Charles is who I am meant to be with for the rest of my life.

"Because Lydia, I don't want to be known as a cheat. Not only that, but I gave up my job and my independence to live with Charles as I thought that he was going to be my happy ending. It hurts that, the more I stay with him, the more I realise that isn't the case. I just need to focus on writing my book and I need to forget about Jake," I reply. She looks at me with a little sadness in her eyes and I just shrug my shoulders. I may not love Charles anymore but it still stings that things haven't worked out the way I hoped that they would. "Actually, the first thing I need to do is go home and see what Charles has to say." I stand and go to the kitchen to get my handbag and laptop.

"Good luck babes," Lydia calls out to me. "And you know that if you need to, you are always welcome to stay here."

"Thanks Lyd," I say, as I poke my head back around the lounge doorway. "I'll call you later." I leave her flat and decide not to shout bye to Donnie as I go. He usually tries to hug me when I leave which makes me cringe. I wish Lydia would see sense as she's far too good for him. I stroll back home slowly as I prepare myself for what I am going to walk into when I get there.

Chapter Eight.

I walk in the front door and the house smells divine. The scent of roast lamb wafts down the hall way. My stomach grumbles in appreciation. I walk through the lounge to go to the dining room and I hear Charles faffing about in the kitchen. Wow, he has really gone to town. The dining table is set, there is soft music playing, candles are lit on the table and the curtains are drawn. The silver ware is making an unexpected appearance, and a bottle of wine sits in a cooler at the end of the table. I call out to Charles to let him know that I am back.

"Oh, okay. If you could sit in the dining room darling, I will bring the food through. Help yourself to a glass of wine whilst you are waiting," Charles replies. *What the fuck is wrong with him? This is not the actions of someone who is going to kick me out of the house, surely?* I put my laptop and handbag on a little table in the corner of the room. I busy myself by pouring some wine for both of us, and then I take a seat and wait. Charles enters the room a few moments later carrying a plate with roast lamb on it. My mouth starts to water. He then goes back to the kitchen and returns to the dining room with all the accompaniments that he has made to go with the lamb. After placing them on the table, he sits opposite me. "Would you like me to serve?" he asks me.

"No, no, I can manage thanks." I sound confused. He must pick up on it as he just sits and stares at me. This is so out of character for him. I put some lamb on my plate, trying to ignore Charles' fixed gaze. It only takes me about thirty seconds before I decide that I cannot sit through a whole meal and deal with his weird behaviour.

"Charles, what the hell is going on? Forgive me for coming across as unappreciative but, you never do anything like this for me. And you certainly don't spend your time staring at me over the dinner table. I don't understand what is with the dramatic change in you?" I look at him and wait for a response. Minutes of tension and silence passes by and then, all of a sudden, Charles starts to cry. *Oh shit, why is he crying? This must be serious.* The only other time I have seen him shed any tears was at his father's funeral. I am unsure whether to comfort him or just stay where I am. I opt for the latter.

"Charles, what the hell is the matter with you? What's happened?" I sound panicky, and to be honest, I need him to talk to me as he is starting to make me feel nervous. My appetite quickly disappears. I wait as Charles tries to calm himself down. After a minute or so he takes a sip of wine, and inhales a few deep breaths. The urge to tell him to hurry up and speak is so strong, but I manage to keep my mouth shut. All the while my mind is racing as I try to figure out what the problem is.

"Stacey, I am so sorry. I need to tell you something," he says in a shaky voice.

"Well, come on then, out with it." I can't help but show the impatience in my voice. He's really panicking me now.

"You know I told you that I stayed at Mummy's last night?" I just nod my head at him. I daren't speak for fear that he will go all quiet on me again. "Well........I didn't......I didn't stay there. I'm so sorry darling, I don't know what came over me." He starts blubbing again.

"Okay," I say, warily. "So, where did you stay?" I start to feel very uncomfortable. I think I know what he is about to say, but I need my suspicions confirmed before I say anything else.

"I went home with Claire, the woman I was talking to. I was so drunk and you had left and I really don't know what came over me," he rambles, quickly. It takes me a few seconds to process his words. He spoke so fast that I am almost convinced that I misheard him. As I stare at the lamb on my plate, which now looks very unappealing, I replay his words in my head. I haven't misheard anything. His behaviour at Danish and the treating me better is just his way of trying to deal with his guilt.

"Please talk to me darling. I need to know what you are thinking," he pleads with me. I lift my eyes from my plate of lamb and look at him. He looks panicked.

"The blonde woman?" I ask.

"Yes."

"So, you went home with this Claire woman and fucked her. Then you come home to me and cook a lovely dinner and break out the fancy plates, which is meant to achieve what exactly? Forgiveness?" My tone is flat in my reply.

"I just...........I just thought that I would do something nice so you would be able to see how sorry I

~ 59 ~

am." His reply is pathetic. He really is an ass. He would have been better off letting me live in ignorant bliss. I mean, we haven't had sex for weeks now so I really couldn't give a toss that he slept with someone else. I would be a hypocrite to start shouting and bawling at him. Lucky for me, he is unaware about my past dalliance. The first thought that springs to mind is, where the hell am I going to live? And what am I going to do for work seeing as I can no longer continue to live here now he has dropped this bombshell. Jeez, I'm not even fazed by the concept of not being with Charles. Surely I should feel some sort of jealousy or anger? I don't though. All I feel at the moment is a mixture of panic and relief. Panic at having to find somewhere else to live with no money, and relief that it's finally over. No longer will I have to play the part of the doting girlfriend. No longer will I have to listen to his mother's snide remarks. Maybe I can finally start to feel good about myself again? Charles speaks, interrupting my thoughts.

"You're not going to leave me, are you? I don't want this to break us Stacey." I don't mean to, but I actually laugh in his face.

"Oh come on Charles, we have been on the rocks for a long time. These last few months especially have solidified just how different we both are."

"But.....but...." I cut him off before he can say anymore.

"I'm going to get some of my things together and go and stay at Lydia's. I can't stay here Charles. We're not good for each other. We just don't fit anymore, and to be honest, I'm not sure if we ever did." He tries to speak again but I just hold my hands up to stop him. "Don't worry about sleeping with Claire. She is probably a much better fit for you than I ever was." With that I stand up, drain my glass of wine, and I go upstairs to pack my bag. As I pack my essentials, the sense of relief washes over me again. My dreams of becoming a writer may be put on hold, but I am finally free. Free of his critique and free to do what the hell I want. I will no longer have to adhere to the weekly meal plan, or to his insistence that I accompany him to all of his boring events. And the best part is that he will have to be the one to tell people why I left him. I smile and head back to the dining room to retrieve my handbag and laptop. Charles is still sat at the table looking gobsmacked.

"Goodbye Charles. I will collect the rest of my stuff in a few days." He doesn't answer me. I turn and feel almost serene as I leave the house. I decide to walk to Lydia's instead of taking my car. I can pick it up when I collect the rest of my stuff. I need a walk to clear my head a bit. It's at times like these that I really do wish that I had some family to turn to. I miss having the security of a family to support me in times of need. I should count myself lucky that I met Lydia really. Without her, I don't know where I would go right now. She is like the sister that I never had. I slowly walk, processing all that has happened. It's been an emotional twenty-four hours that's for sure. I reach Lydia's flat in a daze. I knock on her door for the second time today and I try not to cringe as Donnie answers, wearing only a towel around his waist. *Jeez, does this guy not know where his clothes are?*

"Hey pretty lady," he drools at me.

"Uh, hi. Can I come in?" I ask, as politely as possible.

"Sure." He steps back from the door slightly to let me in. "Lydia is in the lounge recovering from our last sex session." *Ugh, why does he feel the need to announce this to me?* "Going somewhere?" he asks me as his eyes rest on the holdall that I have in my hand.

"Not exactly." I would rather speak to Lydia first before saying anything to Donnie about needing a place to stay. "I'll just go through and see Lyd. Perhaps you could try and wear some clothes whilst I'm here?" Donnie chuckles to himself as I walk through to the lounge. Lydia is led on the sofa watching some crappy day time television. "Hey Lyd."

"Crikey Stace, are you trying to give me a heart attack?" Lydia exclaims as she springs up to a sitting position and holds her hand over her heart for effect. "Don't sneak up on me like that."

"Sorry, I thought that you would have heard me talking to Donnie," I say through my laughter.

"It's not bloody funny," she says with a smirk. Her eyes soon notice the holdall in my hand. "Things didn't go well with Charles then?" I flop down on the sofa next to her and tell her all about what happened when I got back home. Although, I shouldn't think of it as my home anymore because it isn't. She doesn't say anything until I have finished updating her, but when she speaks, all she says is, "about bloody time you left that douche bag."

"I should have guessed that you would be happy."

"Oh Stace, I'm not happy that you have split up...."

"Really?" I interrupt her and give her a knowing look.

"Okay, maybe I am a little happy, but it's only because I know you deserve better than to be treated like someone's maid. I just want you to be happy and I know that you weren't." She has a point. I haven't been truly happy for a long time.

"Can I stay here with you for a few days? I just need to get myself sorted."

"Of course you can stay here, and you can stay for as long as you want."

"Thanks Lyd. I don't know what I would do without you." I am so grateful to this girl. I'm sure Martin would have helped me, but Lydia is always the first person that I turn to. Plus, if Charles were to find out that I was staying with Martin, then I know that he would make Martin's life difficult at work. "Now I have the task of finding a job." I can almost see the cogs turning in Lydia's head.

"Why don't you come back and work at The Den? You know what you're doing, and who better to have as your boss than your best friend, *again?* What do you say? It will be like old times."

"Really? You don't think everyone would be pissed off if I came back?" I feel myself perk up a little at the prospect of finding work so quickly.

"Don't be so bloody stupid. Everyone loved you working there. I will take a look at the shifts when I go in tomorrow and see what I can do," she says with a wink. "As for tonight, get your glad rags on because we are going out to celebrate."

"Oh no, I really don't feel like going out," I tell her. I don't know why I bother though. Once Lydia has her mind set on doing something, there really is no way that she will take no for an answer.

"Bollocks. You're coming out with me and that's final. It's been so long since we went out, not to mention that I get to see single Stacey in action." I roll my eyes at her. I'm really not looking to catch another guy's attention tonight. I think I should just concentrate on myself for a while. "The spare bedroom is all yours babes. Make yourself at home."

"Thanks Lyd." I smile at her. I take my few belongings into the spare bedroom, shutting the door behind me. The room is small with a single bed, wardrobe, chest of drawers and a bedside table. I don't mind it being small though, it makes the room feel cosy. Lydia has decorated it in a pastel yellow colour, which brings a warm vibe to the room. I leave my bags at the end of the bed and set up my laptop on the bedside table. I decide to do some writing to occupy my mind. I get myself settled on the bed and proceed to write for as long as I can, before

Lydia demands that I stop so that I can get ready for our impromptu night out. I have only been writing for ten minutes, when I hear my phone ringing in my handbag. I retrieve my phone and am unsurprised to see that Charles is trying to phone me. I don't even consider answering his call. I put my phone on silent and ignore his attempt to speak to me. Even if I did answer, there would be nothing that he could say to convince me to go back to him. I am just glad that he never found out about Jake. I know Charles, and I know that he would have used it as ammunition to help his current situation. Surely he must agree that we no longer fit together? I can't imagine that he was truly happy with me. Maybe he just liked having me around to be at his beck and call? If Charles had been the one to end things with me, then I am in no doubt that he would never have contacted me again. Maybe his ego has been hurt at how I left him without batting an eyelid? I silently curse myself that it took him admitting that he slept with someone else in order for me to finally leave. In retrospect, I have used him as much as he may have used me. I make a promise to myself right now that I will never again let myself stay in an unhealthy relationship. Life is too short to be unhappy.

Chapter Nine.

A couple of hours pass by, and I have managed to write another two thousand words of my novel. I am pleased with my progress, especially with all the moaning and groaning that I have heard from the bedroom next door. Lydia and Donnie are literally at it like rabbits! I am surprised that Donnie can go so many times. Maybe that's why Lydia sticks with him? I save my work and shut down my laptop. There is a knock on my bedroom door and Lydia enters my room.

"Hey babes. We need to start getting ready to go out." Lydia looks every bit as dishevelled as she did when I first came to see her this morning.

"Was just thinking the same thing. You have finally finished shagging then?"

"Yes thanks." A stupid grin crosses Lydia's face. "Now, get your ass in the shower and get ready. It's already seven o clock and we need to get the drinking started. Help yourself to anything in my wardrobe, as I presume you didn't pack any going out clothes in your rush to get away from the douche bag."

I chuckle. "Thanks Lyd. Are you sure you're not too tired to go out? I mean, it sounds like you have been having quite the workout this afternoon?" I raise one eyebrow at her.

"Number one, I am never too tired to go out. Number two, you shouldn't be eavesdropping. And number three, get a bloody move on." Lydia exits my bedroom before I can respond, shutting the door behind her. I shake my head as I get off of the bed and leave the room. I head to the bathroom to get ready. Unfortunately for me, Donnie is stood in the bathroom doorway. I have to physically stop myself from rolling my eyes at him.

"So, wild night out tonight then? Lydia told me about you and Charles. So sorry to hear that by the way." *Yeah, the use of sarcasm in your tone makes you sound so sincere. Ugh, this guy gives me the creeps.* "Maybe you might be up for some extra special fun later?" He winks at me. I am too shocked by his suggestion to respond, but my face must say it all. "Calm down, I'm only messing about," Donnie laughs. I'm not convinced that he is just joking though. I think that if I said yes to his little proposal, then he would be more than willing to cheat on Lydia. What a slime ball. I push past him and lock myself in the bathroom. With him around, living here may be harder than I thought. I turn on the shower and let the water warm up as I try to erase Donnie's words from my mind. They guy really needs to get a better sense of humour if he calls remarks like that a 'joke.' I get undressed and step into the shower. I take my time, letting the warm water cascade over my body as I replay the day's events in my head. When I woke up this morning, I did not expect any of this to have happened. I feel happy and elated that I have my freedom back. I may possibly have a job, I have the bestest friend ever, and I'm going out tonight to let loose and enjoy myself. Surely nothing else could possibly go wrong? I hear Lydia's voice which breaks through my thoughts.

"Stacey! Get your skinny butt out of the shower and get ready! I've got the drinks waiting." I drag myself out of the shower, dry myself and wrap the towel around me. I then dash to Lydia's bedroom to choose an outfit. I mentally curse myself for not having chosen an outfit before having a shower. The last thing I want is for Donnie to see me in just a towel. Lucky for me, he must be in the lounge or kitchen. I have a rifle through Lydia's wardrobe and come across a pair of small black tailored shorts, which I team with a black sparkly vest top. Charles would never have approved of this outfit, but I love it. I hurry back to my bedroom and put the outfit on. I opt for minimal make-up. I apply beige eyeshadow, a touch of mascara, eyeliner and some clear lip gloss. Perfect. I dry my hair and add in some soft waves. I put on a pair of Lydia's black stilettos; luckily we are the same size in clothes and shoes. I take a look at myself in the hallway mirror and I love the way that I look. The outfit makes me feel sexy and confident. Pleased with my appearance, I head to the lounge where I can hear Lydia and Donnie talking. I enter the lounge and Donnie wolf whistles.

"Looking good Stacey," he leers at me, and his eyes roam over my body. It makes me feel uncomfortable and I contemplate changing into something less revealing, but then I change my mind. I shouldn't let this jack ass stop me from feeling good about myself. Lydia is sat next to him on the sofa. I wonder if she feels as uncomfortable about his comment as I do? It doesn't appear so, as she doesn't seem to bat an eyelid.

"He's right girl. You will be fighting the men off of you." Lydia picks a glass up off of the coffee table and hands it to me.

"I'm not going for the men Lyd; I've only just broken up with Charles." I take the glass from her and take a sip. Gin, lemonade and lime. Delicious.

"So?" Lydia replies. "You should enjoy some attention now that you are finally rid of him. No one is saying that you need to jump straight into another relationship, just live a little." Donnie nods in agreement with her whilst still leering at me. I look away from him and admire my best friends outfit choice. Lydia looks beautiful in her hot pink, strapless jump suit and white stilettos. She has never been one to shy away into the crowd. I notice that Donnie is dressed up too, and this can only mean that he is coming with us. Oh great, I will be playing the part of a gooseberry for most of the night whilst they play tonsil tennis with each other. I can't help feeling a little disappointed that it isn't just Lydia and I going out. The three of us sit chatting and drinking for the next hour. My acting skills are really improving as I manage to speak to Donnie without cringing. When we are ready to leave, I go back to my room to grab my phone off of the bedside table. I notice that I have three missed calls and a text message. They are all from Charles. He hasn't left any voicemails. I open the text message and begin to read.

Stacey, please will you talk to me. I'm so sorry for

what I have done, but you can't leave me! What

will people think? We can sort this out, just come

back and talk to me. Charles x.

And in that one message it shows me the real reason that he's sorry. He's worried about how it will look to everyone else. I scoff and decide not to take my phone out. I switch it off and place it back on the bedside table. I don't want to have my night ruined by receiving anymore messages from him. I grab my little black handbag, put my money inside, take one last look at myself in the mirror, and I am ready to go. The three of us leave the flat and walk to The Den. I can tell that Lydia is half cut already. Ten minutes later and we arrive at our destination. We enter the bar area and I see that Susie is working tonight. As I approach her she screams loudly and comes running over to me to give me a hug.

"Hey hun. I've missed seeing you!" she shouts into my ear drum, nearly deafening me. "Where have you been hiding?"

"Hey Susie," I say whilst giggling. "I haven't been hiding, but I am now free and single, and I am ready to party my ass off."

"Well say no more then. Let me fix you one of my special cocktails." She heads back behind the bar with a wink. For such a small petite woman, Susie is very loud. She looks cute with her blonde hair cropped into a pixie style haircut. Lydia and Donnie join me at the bar as Susie is bringing me my drink. She quickly goes and whips them up the same. The drink is divine and tastes of raspberries more than anything else. I moan my approval and signal for her to make me another one. I drain the second drink as quickly as the first and grab Lydia's hand to go and dance. I literally pull her off of the bar stool that she is sat on and drag her behind me.

"Whoa, calm down babes. You nearly pulled my arm out of its socket."

"Sorry. I just feel so alive and I need my dancing partner to help me out." We dance for what feels like ages. There are a few guys I have to tell to back off as I don't want their attention. Tonight is all about celebrating new beginnings and leaving the past behind. Eventually Donnie joins us on the dancefloor and I excuse myself to go to the toilet. I feel his eyes watching me as I walk away and it makes my skin crawl. I finish up in the toilets and decide that I will get myself another of Susie's amazing cocktails before doing anymore dancing. As I exit the ladies, Donnie is waiting outside for me. I instantly panic that something is wrong with Lydia.

"Is everything okay Don? Where's Lydia?" I ask, worried.

"Everything's fine. Lydia's getting some more drinks at the bar. I thought that I would come and make sure you were alright."

"I'm fine. Why wouldn't I be?" I may be a little bit drunk but I'm perfectly capable of getting to the toilets and back by myself. Donnie closes the space between us and grabs my arm. Before I have the chance to say anything, he leads me down a small corridor next to the ladies' toilets. "Donnie, what the fuck are you doing?" I shout at him.

"Ssssshhhh." He says as he pushes me up against the wall and places his finger over my lips. I feel panic start to overtake all of my senses. "I have been waiting to get you alone all night. You look sexy as hell, and I know you want me just as much as I want you." *What the fuck?! Has he gone insane?* This guy really does think that he is god's gift to women. His hand grips my waist and the other is playing with a ringlet of my hair. I try to calm my breathing.

"Donnie, I don't know what's going on here, but I have no interest in you in that way. You are with Lydia and I tolerate you for *her* sake. If it were up to me, she would have kicked your ass to the curb a long time ago." I speak as confidently as I can, but the nerves in my voice betray me. I stare straight at him as I try to prise his hand from my waist. The more I try to prise his fingers off of me, the tighter his grip gets. "Donnie, get your hands off of me. I'm not interested."

"You always have been a fucking tease Stacey." His tone has changed to one of anger. He pins me to the wall with his body, stops playing with my hair, and holds my hands above my head with one of his hands, and I feel the other hand leave my waist and start to stroke the top of my thigh. I try to wriggle free, but he is just too strong for me. My eyes widen and I can feel the onset of tears as I desperately try not to show him that I am frightened.

"Donnie, please get off of me. I don't want this." I plead with him, but he's not listening. Fear envelopes me as I feel his hand shift and he grazes the inside of my thigh with his fingers. *Oh my god, he's going to assault me. He's going to assault me here in The Den.* No one knows that he has brought me down this corridor, and with the music loud, no one will be able to hear me scream. I continue to try and jerk him away with my body, but he just pushes his body into me so much that I almost feel like I can't breathe. I am trapped. I can feel my stomach churning. My heartbeat is racing and I am desperately trying to figure out how to get myself out of this situation and away from this man.

"Donnie, get the fuck off of me NOW!" I scream at him again and again, but he's still not stopping. I feel like I might pass out at any moment. As his hand moves upwards and brushes my sex, I suddenly hear a voice.

"Get the fuck off of her, *now.*" Oh my god, someone has come to save me. Thank fuck for that. A feeling of recognition rushes through me at the voice that has spoken. I feel Donnie's grip on my hands loosen slightly. His other hand moves back to my waist, but his grip is still firm. He turns his head in the direction of the voice at the same time as I do. Jake is standing there with his fists balled at his sides, and he looks all shades of pissed off. I feel immense relief at seeing him standing there. I can see the menace in his eyes, which are fixated on Donnie.

"And what are you gonna do about it?" Donnie goads.

"You don't want to find out, believe me. Now get your filthy hands off of her and I'll let you walk out of here with your face still in one piece." Jake's voice is like ice. Donnie looks back to me and smirks.

"She wants this just as much as I do mate. Now why don't you piss off and leave us to it?" Donnie says as he looks back to Jake. My eyes plead with Jake to stay where he is. Jake however is keeping his gaze on Donnie. I hold my breath as I will Donnie to let go of me.

"I'm going nowhere. Now let her go." He pronounces each word slowly. I almost whimper at Jake's answer. *He's not going anywhere. He's going to help me.*

"For fuck sake," Donnie says as he lets go of me and turns to face Jake. My legs give way and I collapse onto the floor as the tears that I have been holding back start to fall from my eyes. I move myself along the floor and as far back from Donnie as I can. I see Donnie move towards Jake, but he's not quick enough. Jake launches himself and punches Donnie in the face. Donnie falls to the ground where Jake proceeds to punch him in the face, repeatedly. Donnie is shouting at Jake to get off of him but it's like Jake has completely lost it. I need to do something and quick, before Jake puts Donnie in a coma, or worse.

"Jake!" I shout. "Jake, please don't. He's not worth it. Please stop." I sob as the tears continue to fall. My voice has an impact as Jake looks at me. He has Donnie pinned to the floor, his arm across Donnie's neck. "Please Jake," I whisper as a last attempt to get him to let go of Donnie. He registers my words, although how he hears me over the background music, I'm not quite sure. Jake takes his eyes off of me and looks back to Donnie.

"If you ever go near Stacey again, I will kill you. Understand?" Jake's voice is laced with venom. Donnie just nods his head. He looks petrified. "And if you ever tell anyone what I did to you, your pathetic existence won't be worth living. Understand?" Again Donnie just nods. Blood covers Donnie's face, but I don't feel sorry for him. How could I ever feel sorry for someone like him? I dread to think about how far Donnie would have gone if Jake hadn't shown up when he did. Jake stands up, releasing his grip on Donnie, and picks me up in his arms as if I weigh nothing more than the weight of a feather. Jake carries me past Donnie and out into the main room of The Den. I bury my face in Jake's chest so that no one can see that I have been crying. The last thing I need is Lydia or Susie spotting me and asking questions about what's wrong. We walk through the main room undetected, and straight out of the front doors. It is only when the fresh air hits me that I turn my head to see where Jake is taking me. I see Jake's limo parked across the road from The Den. There is a man leant against it, and I assume it is Eric as I didn't actually see what he looked like the last time I was with Jake. When he sees us approaching, he opens the door and Jake slides me in first, and then climbs in after me. I sit on the plush leather seats but I feel no comfort this time. I feel numb. As Eric gets back into the driver's seat, Jake puts his arms around me and pulls me onto his lap. I can feel my body shaking and my tears keep flowing.

"Sssshhh, it's okay baby. I've got you. No one will hurt you again." Jake speaks softly as he places a kiss on the top of my head. His words make me feel safe. I cling to him. I don't want him to let go of me. I don't ask where we are going, and I don't really care either. I am far too dazed to concentrate on anything but the feel of Jake's arms holding me. This was supposed to be my night, my new beginning, and my celebration. Now it just feels like my world is ending.

Chapter Ten.

I manage to stop crying as the limo pulls to a stop. Jake gently slides me off of his lap and tilts my chin up to look at him.

"It's okay. You're safe. I'm going to look after you." He cups my face in both of his hands and gently wipes my cheeks with his thumbs. He wipes away the remainder of the last of my tears. The act is so unexpected that I almost start crying again from how gentle he is being with me. I don't have the energy to argue with him about letting him look after me. I let him take my hand and lead me out of the limo. Jake turns to Eric, who is stood by the limo.

"Thanks Eric. Take the day off tomorrow. I will be working from home."

"Yes sir," Eric replies. Eric is an older guy with greying hair, but he is huge. He must be in his fifties, and his shirt can barely contain his muscles. He must be at least six foot in height, if not more. "Goodnight to you both." I manage a feeble smile to acknowledge him. My eyes wander from Eric to the impressive building in front of us. It is massive. From the outside there appears to be three floors. The house is detached and is surrounded by a six-foot-high red brick wall. Flowers line the steps up to the front door, and hanging baskets show an array of colourful flowers. We are stood on a large gravel covered drive way. I look behind me and see that Eric has returned to the limo and is reversing back out onto the road.

"Where am I?" I ask.

"You're staying at mine tonight," Jake says in a firm tone. I fall silent as I let him lead me up the few steps to the front door. Once Jake has opened the front door, he takes me down a long, spacious hall way and only stops when we reach a door at the very end. He opens the door and leads me into the biggest kitchen that I have ever seen. Beautiful oak cabinets line the back wall of the room, and the black granite worktops sparkle as if they are brand new. For all I know, they could be brand new. There is a kitchen island in the middle of the room with two bar stools on one side. To the right of me there are a set of impressive French doors. I don't know what the doors lead out to as it is pitch black outside so I can't see anything. To my left is a stunning black aga and more granite worktops housing different kitchen equipment. I turn slightly and see that behind me is an American sized fridge. It must cost a fortune to fill it up with food. I feel like I have walked into a show home. Jake clears his throat which draws my attention back to him. My eyes connect with his and he gestures for me to take a seat on one of the bar stools. I oblige as I suddenly feel tired. As I sit, I think about how this room alone is bigger than Lydia's entire flat. *Oh my god! Lydia!* She has no idea what her boyfriend has done to me tonight.

"Jake, I need to see my friend, Lydia. I need to speak to her. I can't let Donnie get to her first." The last thing I need is Donnie telling her some cock and bull story that he has concocted. Saying his name leaves a bitter taste in my mouth. I start to feel panicky that she may be left alone with him at some point. "Oh god, what if he tries to hurt her too?" My mind is in overdrive now. I feel sick at the thought.

"Don't worry, I have asked someone to get a message to her to let her know that you are safe," he says as he hands me a glass of water. I gratefully take a sip as my mouth is so dry.

"How the hell have you managed that? And how do you know who Lydia is?" He's been with me since it all happened and I can't recall him talking to anyone.

"It doesn't matter how. The important thing is she knows that you are safe. I just want to make sure that you are okay. Don't worry, she will get home safely. I promise." I don't quite know what to say. He seems to have taken care of everything.

"Thank you. I appreciate you helping me back there. God knows how far he would have gone if……." I shudder as I recall Donnie's hands touching my body.

"Don't think about that now. I think it's best that you get some sleep. We can sort everything out when you are rested." Jake takes my hand. "Come, I will show you the guest bedroom." I hop off of the bar stool, follow him back into the hall way, and up a set of stairs. We go up one flight of stairs and then we continue up a second flight before we reach a long corridor. There are only two doors. One on each side of the corridor. Jake takes me into the room on the right. I enter a large, and very plush looking bedroom. The bed is gigantic; I've never seen anything like it. You could probably fit half a dozen full grown adults in it and still have some room left. Jake tells me that the door to the left of the room leads to an ensuite, and the door on the right leads to a walk in wardrobe and a dressing room. A big flat screen television is on the wall at the end of the bed, with a beautiful decorative fireplace underneath. My jaw drops open at how vast and luxurious the room is. The bed looks very inviting, and all I want to do is disappear beneath the covers. I feel a little shaky and presume that the adrenaline and shock, from what happened, has started to subside a little.

"My bedroom is across the hall if you need me. There are some pyjama's in the ensuite but, uh, they are a pair of mine. I don't have anything else but I figure that you may like to wear something comfortable to sleep in."

"That's great, thanks." He is being so sweet. "Are you sure I'm not imposing on you?" I ask, hoping that he won't say yes. To be honest, I wouldn't feel safe going back to Lydia's tonight.

"Of course not. Treat it as you would your own bedroom, and please try to get some rest." Jake kisses my forehead and then leaves the bedroom, shutting the door on his way out. I wrap my arms around myself and scan the room again. It's like I'm stood in a room out of a catalogue. It is beautiful. I head to the walk in wardrobe, open the doors, and take a look inside. The rails are all empty except for the pair of pyjamas that Jake said that I could wear. To the left of the rails there is a dressing table that has nothing but a hairdryer on it. I take the pyjamas and head in the opposite direction of the room to the ensuite. I come to a standstill in the ensuite hall way as I see that there is a walk in shower taking up a quarter of the space, a big oval shaped bath tub in the middle of the room, and a toilet and two sinks at the other end. *Wow, this guy really knows how to design a guest room. All I need is a kitchen and I'm set!* I quickly strip myself of the clothes I am wearing, which I throw into a bin in the corner of the room. I will replace them for Lydia. I just can't bear to look at them. I turn on the shower and wait for the water to heat up, which takes all of a few seconds. There is shampoo, conditioner and body wash on a small shelf to the left of the shower head. The urge to scrub my body is overwhelming. The feel of Donnie's hands on my body makes me retch. I scrub and scrub my skin until it becomes too sore to scrub anymore. I turn off the shower and dry myself on a mammoth sized towel. The towel is warm as it has been hanging on a heated rail just outside of the shower cubicle. I pull on the pyjama top and put the matching bottoms on. The bottoms are too big, but I tuck the top into them to help keep them up as best as I can. I head to the sink to see if I can find a toothbrush to brush my teeth. I look in the mirror above the sink and see that I really do look bloody awful. My face is pale and I look like I have aged about ten years. I sigh as I contemplate my reflection and then let my eyes wander to a cabinet just to the right of the mirror, which I open to find everything that I could possibly need. It's vanity heaven in here. I find a toothbrush as well as a hairbrush and hair ties on the bottom shelf, all still in their packaging. I undo the packaging for the toothbrush and clean my teeth. I then use the hairbrush to brush my hair and tie it into a ponytail before my mind drifts off to how Lydia is. I hope that she is okay. I can't lose her, she's my best friend. I just hope she believes me when I tell her what happened. I sigh, putting the hairbrush back in the cabinet. I exit the ensuite and climb into the bed. I sink into the mattress. As I lie there, I torture myself by replaying the events of what happened tonight over and over again, until eventually, sleep takes over.

Chapter Eleven.

I wake up to be greeted with a pounding headache. I sit up in bed, and for a few moments, I wonder where the hell I am. Then I remember how Jake brought me to his place. The horrendous events of last night flood my brain. I have to run to the bathroom as I feel the bile rising in my throat. Once I finish emptying the remaining contents of my stomach, I brush my teeth and wash my face. I still look pale, but that's hardly surprising really. I decide to head downstairs and see if I can find Jake. I notice that it is only just gone eight in the morning. At least I have managed to get a few hours' sleep, even though it doesn't feel like it. I leave my room and go to the stairs, only to hear Jake's voice coming from the floor below. I freeze and decide to listen. I know that I shouldn't be eavesdropping but I don't want to interrupt anything.

"What part aren't you getting? I don't want you back and I never will. Now please stop phoning me Caitlin, before I take out a restraining order." Jake goes quiet and I presume that he is done with his conversation. I wonder who this Caitlin woman is whilst I descend the stairs. Then again, it's not really any of my business. Jake is just being kind to me after witnessing what happened last night. I just need to be grateful for his help and not read too much into his actions. I walk down the stairs and see that Jake isn't in the hall way, meaning he must be in one of the rooms. I continue to head down to the kitchen so that I don't disturb him. I reach the kitchen and decide a coffee needs to be my first port of call. I busy myself trying to find a cup. When I have located one, about four cupboards later, I spot the coffee machine on the far left worktop. I press the button for an Americano and let the machine do its work. As the coffee filters into the cup, I breath in the aroma of the coffee beans. It smells divine. Once the machine has finished, I take my cup and move to the sink to add a touch of cold water so that I can drink it straight away. I take my first sip, lean against the granite work top, and close my eyes at how delicious the coffee tastes. I let out a small moan of approval and almost drop the cup when I hear, "morning. Glad to see you're making yourself at home." My eyes fly open and my heart hammers inside my chest.

"Christ you scared me," I say, as I put my hand over my beating heart.

"Sorry, I didn't mean to scare you," Jake replies. He smirks as he says it though so I would say he is more amused by my reaction than he is sorry.

"It's okay. Um, I just needed some coffee. I hope that's okay?" Shit, maybe I should have asked him if it was okay first? What if he thinks that he won't be able to get rid of me now? The last thing that I would want him to think is that I would outstay my welcome.

"Relax, it's fine." His playful tone makes me smile and butterflies start to dance around my stomach. "Nice pyjamas by the way," he says with a mischievous look in his eyes.

"Oh, uh, yeah. Thanks for letting me use them." I smile at him shyly.

"Would you like some breakfast?" he asks me.

"Oh no, I'm good with just the coffee thanks."

"No, you need to eat. I whip up a mean omelette, or there are fresh pastries in the box on the side." He points to where the box is sitting. I really don't feel like eating anything but I don't want to be appear rude, so I go over to the box and take out a croissant. I take the first bite and it tastes good. Really good. In fact, it's so delicious that it doesn't take me long to finish eating it. "Taste good?" Jake asks as he picks out a pain au chocolate for himself.

"Delicious. Thank you." I sit on one of the bar stools and sip my coffee. Jake sits beside me and finishes off his food. He looks divine in his white tank top and grey jogging bottoms with his hair all in disarray. His caramel eyes burn into mine. His very presence overwhelms me.

"How are you feeling this morning?" he asks, concern etched all over his face.

"To be honest, I don't really know. I just need to speak to Lydia and see how she is." She is one of the only constants in my life and I really can't lose her friendship.

"She will be here at two o clock to speak to you," Jake says as if it's no big deal. I nearly spit out the mouthful of coffee that I have just taken.

"Pardon?"

"She's coming here at two. I had a message sent to her this morning and I have arranged for Eric to pick her up to come and see you." He looks completely unfazed. I on the other hand probably look ridiculous with the faces I am pulling.

"Hold on. How did you know where to find her?"

"Now that is something that I can't share with you. Top secret I'm afraid." He winks at me and his playful tone is back, but I am a little freaked out.

"No seriously, how do you know where she lives?" I need to know that he isn't some deranged stalker.

"I had a friend escort her home from The Den last night to make sure she got home safely. Actually, I think the friend ended up staying the night with her, if the squealing in the background was anything to go by." Jake looks a little uncomfortable at the thought. I can't help but burst out laughing. Jake's eyes go wide as he watches me giggling hysterically.

"I'm sorry, it's just your face is such a picture."

"I'm glad that I amuse you," he smiles. Once I have managed to calm down from my laughing fit, I open my mouth to ask him if Lydia knows anything about last night, but before I can do so he cuts me off.

"She doesn't know anything about what happened." *How did he know I was going to ask that?*

"What are you, a mind reader?"

"No, just good at reading people." He stares at me intently. I break the gaze and get up from my stool to get myself another coffee. "It's not anyone else's place to tell her what happened."

"Thank you," I say as I smile at his thoughtfulness. A dark thought suddenly crosses my mind. "Hey, wait a minute. You beat the shit out of Donnie, aren't you worried that he will report you?" I ask. I start to worry what repercussions Jake may face for helping me.

"Not worried in the slightest. You will not be hearing from him again and neither will I. And if he has any sense then he won't be bothering Lydia again either." *Fuck, did he do something else to him?* Jake sees the look on my face and instantly shuts down my thoughts. "Stop worrying. It's a guy thing. He just knows not to come near you ever again and that's all you need to know." Once again he appears completely unfazed.

"Well……okay then." I can't think of any other response. I lean against the work top and stare into my coffee trying to look for answers. Why did Donnie do it? Why didn't I see it coming?

"Stop worrying," Jake says. He walks over to me and takes my coffee cup from my hands, places it on the work top behind me, and puts his arms around me. I automatically put my arms around his waist. "And stop over thinking. Everything is going to be fine." His words bring me comfort, and the feel of his arms enveloping me put my body at ease. We stand like that for some time, in silence. I am enjoying the closeness too much to think about how strange it is that we are embracing like we have been lovers for years. It should feel strange, hugging a virtual stranger, but it doesn't. In the very little time that I have known Jake, I can honestly say that I have never viewed him as a stranger. He almost feels like home to me. I try to distract from my thoughts of Jake, and I begin to ponder over what may happen when Lydia comes over. What if she doesn't believe me? My eyes flick up to the clock on the wall. The time is 9:13am. I have plenty of time to get ready for Lydia to arrive. I may just take a long hot bath and wear my comfortable clothes. *Clothes! Shit!* I pull away from Jake as I realise that I have no clothes to wear.

"Um, Jake. I have no clothes to wear for when Lydia gets here," I say shyly, pulling my head back to look at him.

"That's not a problem with me," he says with a wink. I playfully smack him on the chest and he laughs. "Don't worry, I have someone collecting your things from Charles' house as we speak."

"WHAT?" I shout as I break my hands from around his waist and lean back. His arms drop to his sides, and he looks a little uncomfortable at my outburst. "Uh, I hope that isn't a problem. I just thought that you may need your personal items whilst you are here."

"Jake, I appreciate the gesture but it's a bit much. I would have made do with these pyjama bottoms and one of your clean t-shirts. Oh my god, Charles is going to flip when he finds out where I am. I really don't need the grief from him right now." I am exasperated. What Jake is doing for me is too much. I mean, bringing me back to his and looking after me is one thing, then making sure I see Lydia is another, but getting me my stuff from my ex-boyfriend's house is insane. That's a lot for some guy that I hardly know to do for me. What reason does he have for doing this? My mind starts to race. *Oh god, what have I gotten myself into by staying here? How does he even know that my stuff is still at Charles' house?*

"I quite like the thought of you in one of my t-shirts," Jake says, trying to lighten my mood. I roll my eyes and give a little groan. "I just thought that I was helping. I would like you to feel comfortable whilst you are here. I thought having your own things would help do that. Plus, Charles has no reason to know I sent the guys who are collecting your things. For all he knows, they could be friends of yours." Jake looks a little offended and I instantly feel guilty.

"Oh god Jake, I didn't mean to sound so ungrateful. It's just all so overwhelming. The last twenty-four hours have been crazy. My head is all over the place and I don't know how to process everything."

"I know. That's why I wanted to make things easier for you." He seems so genuine and my gut is telling me to trust and believe him.

"Thank you," I say, giving him a little smile.

"No problem." He flashes me his heart stopping grin. My knees feel weak. How does he have this effect over me? After what happened last night though, I am so glad that Jake isn't trying to make a move on me. He may be hot, but my confidence has been severely shaken. The doorbell rings, making me jump. Jake leaves the kitchen to go and answer the door. I finish my coffee before following him to the front door. The sight before me is a little more than I expected. There are boxes everywhere. It literally looks like all of my stuff has been brought here. *Shit, I assumed he meant that he was having a few items of clothes collected for me, not my entire life!*

"Um, Jake?" He turns around to look at me. "Why is it that every item I appear to own is sitting, in boxes, in your hall way?"

"I told you that I was having your stuff collected."

"Yes but I thought you meant a few clothes, I didn't realise you meant everything that I own." I am gobsmacked.

"Well, this way, you have no need to go back to Charles' to collect your belongings. Except for your car. Charles is adamant that he can't find the keys. We can go and get it in the next day or two." Jake doesn't bat an eyelid at how insane all of this is. He shakes hands with the guys who have delivered my stuff and closes the door as they leave. "I will take all of this up to the guest room for you," he says, gesturing to the boxes.

"Whoa, hold on a minute mister." Jake gives me a puzzled look. "How long do you think I am staying for?"

"As long as you need to." Well, fuck me, he's only gone and moved me in.

"I don't think that's appropriate Jake. We hardly know each other. I am so grateful to you for everything you have done so far, but I can't live here." Doesn't he see how ridiculous this is?

"Look, before you start getting worried, I am happy for you to stay here." I go to speak, but he raises his finger to stop me as he continues to talk. "I want to help you Stacey. There is no ulterior motive here. I hope that by now you have realised that I am not some raving lunatic. You may come and go as you please, and you may use the house as you would your own place. I am out most of the time due to my work commitments, so you may as well take advantage of the situation. I feel like we have a connection, and I would like to pursue that." My eyebrows raise and Jake quickly corrects his wording. "I mean, I feel that we are starting to become friends, and that thought makes me happy." I feel myself start to soften at his words. "I don't let many people into my life Stacey. I have trusted people before and they have let me down, but when I do sense a connection with someone, I like to explore that connection."

"But…….but…….but I don't have a job, and I wouldn't be able to contribute to the bills or anything." *Oh my god, am I actually considering this?*

"Does it look like that bothers me?"

"Well it bothers me! I don't want people to think that I am using you for your money." *Yep, looks like I am considering this crazy idea!*

"I don't give a fuck what other people think," Jake says, his tone tells me that I should just drop this conversation, but I can't.

"I don't know Jake. It's all so rushed and sudden. This is a big decision, and like I said before, we hardly know each other. I'm also meant to be staying with Lydia." Although, depending on how this afternoon goes, I may not be able to stay with her anyway.

"Well, you have the option to stay here if you need to," Jake responds. We stand in the hall way staring at each other. This is just more information to process in my overloaded brain. I don't have the energy to talk this out right now.

"I'll think about it." This is the only answer that I can give right now.

"Okay then. You think about it and I will start to take these boxes to your room." I don't fail to notice how it has gone from the 'guest room' to 'your room.' "Oh and just for the record, it doesn't feel like we hardly know each other. Not to me anyway." With that, Jake starts to move my boxes from the hall way as I look on in disbelief. Living here with Jake Waters would be luxurious, I have no doubt about that, but can I really do that? Could me living here actually work? My life has gone from zero miles per hour to one hundred in a very short space of time. Mid thought, I pick up one of the smaller boxes and start to take it up the stairs. I am halfway up when Jake startles me, making me drop the box I was holding. I hope there was nothing valuable in there as it could well be broken now.

"What do you think you are doing?" he asks me. I am about to respond, but Jake cuts me off before I can reply. "Don't even think about lifting anything else up here, the boxes are way too heavy."

"Jake, I'm perfectly fine to bring some stuff up here." I roll my eyes at him.

"It's not up for discussion. If you want to help then I would love another cup of coffee, black with one sugar."

"Is this what it would be like if I lived here? Will I be allowed to do anything?" I mock.

"Of course you will. But if it involves carrying heavy items, then that is my job not yours. Now, where are we on that cup of coffee?" I salute Jake as he continues up the stairs chuckling to himself.

"Coming right up sir," I respond playfully before I return to the kitchen. Maybe I could get used to being looked after like this…………..

Chapter Twelve.

I take a quick shower, so much for a long bath, and spend the next hour looking through my boxes trying to find what clothes to wear. I opt for some black leggings, pink vest top and my favourite jumper, which is off the shoulder and baggy, meaning it is comfy. I dry my hair and style it into a side plait that hangs loosely over my shoulder. I don't bother applying make-up. I'm not in the mood to be all dolled up right now. My eyes still look a little puffy from last night, but I don't care about covering it up. I think that seeing Lydia is only going to spark more emotion, so make-up would be a waste of time. I hear the doorbell ring and I head out of the bedroom and downstairs to see if it is Lydia. Jake has already answered the door and is chatting with a guy who has his arm around Lydia's shoulders. *So that must be who escorted Lydia home.* He is tall with an athletic build, green eyes and short blonde, cropped hair. Lydia looks up and sees me coming down the stairs. As I reach the bottom she comes over and pulls me into a massive bear hug. I am shaking when she hugs me, but she doesn't seem to notice.

"So, you dirty stop out, this is where you got to huh? I wondered where the hell you had disappeared to, until this nice young gentleman came and told me," she says as she points to the guy talking to Jake.

"Uh, yeah. It's a long story," I reply.

"I bet it is, and I want to hear every little detail." Lydia doesn't even bother to keep her voice quiet. Jake stops talking to his friend and stares at me as I try to stop myself from crumbling here on the spot. I am struggling to find words.

"Why don't you ladies go through to the lounge, just on the right through that door. You can talk more privately in there." He nods at the relevant door and I mouth my thanks to him. He smiles back and my heart does a little flutter. "Come on Paul, let's leave them to it and go grab a beer."

"Cool," says the guy, who I now know is called Paul. The guys walk off in the direction of the kitchen as Lydia and I head to the lounge. I haven't seen the lounge yet so I have no idea what it looks like. I open the door and just look around the room. It is beautiful, but not as big as I expected it to be. The fact that the lounge is small means it gives it a cosy and warm vibe. The colour scheme is lovely, and the floor is covered in a rich cream carpet that is so plush my feet sink into it. The walls are painted cream but there is a feature wall that is painted in a glorious gold colour. Fresh flowers sit in a vase on the ornate mantelpiece, and a gigantic television literally covers one of the walls opposite the seating area. The seating area consists of a cream coloured corner sofa and a little coffee table in front of it. Jake really does have great taste when it comes to decorating a house. Each room I have seen so far has been stunning.

"Fucking hell Stace, you hit the jackpot when you met him," Lydia says as she strides in and takes a seat on the sofa. "Oh god, this is like bliss on your butt cheeks." I giggle at her comment. I go and sit next to her and take her hand in mine. "Stace?" her face looks puzzled. "What's going on?" I take a deep breath and try to calm my nerves.

"Lyd, I need to tell you something, and I need you to let me get to the end of this before you say anything."

"Come on Stacey, out with it. You're scaring me."

"Something happened to me at The Den last night. I wish I didn't have to tell you this, but..........." I take another deep breath before carrying on. Lydia is staring at me with wide eyes. I need to get this over with. "Donnie tried to assault me." Lydia doesn't move a muscle. She seems to have frozen at my words. "He was waiting for me outside the ladies toilets when I came out. I started to panic as I thought that something had happened to you, for him to be waiting for me." I fight back the tears that are threatening to break through my strength. "After assuring me that you were okay, he grabbed me and led me down the corridor next to the toilets. He shoved me against the wall. I couldn't move Lydia, he had me pinned. I tried to fight him off, but he was too strong. He touched me, and I was screaming at him to get off of me, but he wasn't listening. If it wasn't for Jake showing up when he did, I think he would have........." my voice breaks and I can't bring myself to finish the sentence. Tears start to sting the backs of my eyes, but I need to keep talking. "I'm so sorry Lyd. I never thought that I would ever have to tell you anything like this. I know this must be a shock........" Lydia scoffs and I look at her in surprise.

"Donnie wouldn't do that to me, what are you talking about?" Lydia removes her hand from mine, stands up and starts to pace the room.

"He did, and I wish to god that he hadn't. It breaks me to have to tell you this. You are my best friend Lyd. I need to know that you have understood what I have just told you." Lydia stops pacing and turns to face me.

"Oh I understand. I understand perfectly." There is a tone to her voice that she has never used with me before. "What I don't understand though is why you didn't tell me last night? Why didn't you come straight to me and tell me?" She looks hurt.

"I'm sorry Lyd. I was a mess. Jake had to physically carry me out of the place. I had no idea that he was bringing me here. I was scared and he made me feel safe."

"Oh I bet he did," Lydia's voice is laced with sarcasm.

"It's not like that Lydia." I feel defensive at her insinuation. "Jake has been nothing but kind and he doesn't expect anything in return."

"But *I* am your best friend. You should have been able to come to *me!*" Lydia raises her voice. I knew this wouldn't exactly be a happy conversation, but I did expect her to show some concern. I start to feel anger rise within me.

"You *are* my best friend, but Donnie is the guy that you have been shagging for the last three months. How would I have been able to tell you? He would have made sure that I wouldn't have had the opportunity to."

"You could have at least tried, but instead you let some guy that you barely know bring you to his place. Is this why Donnie ditched me at The Den? Is this why Jake's friend took me home?" I can't answer her, but then I don't really think I need to. I think the answers to those questions are fairly obvious after what I have just told her. "I need to get out of here. I can't be near you right now." Lydia turns to leave the room. Panic surges through me.

"Lyd, please don't go. We need to talk about this." I jump up off of the sofa and follow her into the hall way. Lydia doesn't stop, and she doesn't turn around. I watch as she walks out of the front door, slamming it behind her. I let myself sink to the floor as I watch my best friend walk out of my life. I replay the conversation with Lydia back in my head, and I try to figure out if I could have handled it better. I don't think there is a right way that I could have told her. There is no way that I could have kept it from her. She needed to know the truth about what happened. Not telling her was never an option. I slowly stand, on shaky legs, and go to the mirror in the hall way. I look at my reflection and I don't recognise the person staring back at me. I look pale and my eyes have lost any sparkle that they may have held before. My whole body starts to shake uncontrollably and sheer exhaustion takes over. I'm so tired. I can't face seeing Jake at the moment, so I head for the guest bedroom so that I can be alone with my thoughts. I walk in a daze until I reach the bed. I curl up into a ball on the bed, with my back to the door and I close my eyes. Emotions are rife within me and I don't know how to dissect all that I am feeling. I hate Donnie for what he has done. I despise men who make women feel powerless. I feel used, I feel angry, and I feel lost. I am lost. I have no home, no job, no family, and it looks like I have lost my best friend. Everything is whirring around in my head so quickly that I don't notice that Jake has entered the room until he sits behind me on the bed. He doesn't say anything and I don't turn to look at him. I feel his weight shift as he lies down behind me and puts his arm around me. He just holds me and I let my tears silently flow. I don't attempt to move away from him because his touch brings me comfort. I am hurting and right now, I will take any little bit of comfort that I can get.

Chapter Thirteen.

I open my eyes to a darkened room. I must have fallen asleep. I feel behind me but Jake isn't there. I turn over, reach for the bedside lamp and turn it on. The time on the alarm clock reads 03:42am. I have been asleep for about twelve hours. I feel groggy as I head to the ensuite and use the facilities. I choose to avoid looking at myself in the mirror. I already know that I must look awful without having to see it. My mouth feels dry so I decide to head downstairs to get a drink. I quietly tip toe along the hall way and down the first flight of stairs as I don't want to make any noise. I presume Jake is asleep and I don't want to wake him. I only make it to the first floor though, when I hear voices coming from along the hall way. *Voices at this time of night?* I freeze and turn my head in the direction of the noise. The voices are faint, as they appear to be in one of the rooms, so I tip toe along the hall way a bit in order to hear what is being said.

"What the fuck is wrong with you Jake?" a woman's voice says. Whoever she is, she sounds agitated.

"Nothing is wrong with me," I hear him sigh. "I just don't want you here. Now please will you leave."

"I'm not going anywhere until you explain why you are doing this to me. I love you Jake and we are good together. Why won't you just accept that?" The woman now sounds desperate. I suck in a breath of air as I wait to see what Jake's response will be.

"For Christ sake Caitlin, we are not good together. I don't know how else I can sugar coat this, so I'm just going to be blunt. You are crazy. The only reason I indulged you for so long is because I didn't want you completely losing it. I don't love you, and I never have." This doesn't sound like the Jake that I have come to know. I know I shouldn't be listening, but I can't just walk away now.

"Jake, baby, please don't do this to us. I am not crazy. I just love you so much." The woman, whom I now know is called Caitlin, starts to cry.

"Oh for fuck sake Caitlin, don't you think that turning up at my home at three in the morning is just a little bit strange? I don't want to hurt you, but you are just so infuriating. I am telling you that nothing is going to happen with us anymore, and it never will again. I made a massive mistake by ever sleeping with you in the first place." He sounds mad. *Shit, is this the real Jake?* I barely know the guy. What if the nice Jake is all an act? I quietly tip toe back along the hall way and upstairs, to return to my bedroom, as I don't want to listen to any more of their conversation. My heart is racing as I try to figure out what to do next. I need to leave here. The way he spoke to that woman was horrendous. I definitely won't be able to go back to sleep now. I reach my room and sit on the bed, my mind racing with what options I have. *Who am I kidding, I have no options.* My thoughts are quickly interrupted by the sound of something smashing downstairs. *Oh my god, what the hell was that? Do I go and see? Do I pretend that I am still asleep?* My feet seem to make the decision for me as I stand up off of the bed and head back out into the hall way. This may be one of the worst decisions ever, but I need to see what's happened. I hear the front door slam shut as I reach the first floor. I then hear a grunt coming from one of the rooms. I gingerly walk down the hall way and reach the door that is open slightly. It's Jake's office by the looks of it. My heart is beating wildly as I push the door open fully. As the door opens, Jake comes into view. He's stood clutching his arm, which is covered in blood. My eyes go wide and my mouth drops open at the sight.

"Oh fuck!" I can't help the words escaping from my mouth. Jake looks up at me and I can see fear in his eyes. I quickly rush over to him to take a look at the damage to his arm. There is a large slash mark going down his forearm, and a broken vase lays scattered all over the floor. "What the hell happened in here Jake?" I ask, panic evident in my tone.

"I just knocked the vase and cut myself," Jake answers through gritted teeth. *Really? This is the best excuse that he can come up with?*

"That's bullshit and you know it." However, I don't have time to quiz him on the matter right now. "Wait here. I'll go and grab some towels and then I'm taking you to the hospital." I don't give Jake time to respond as I race out of his office and upstairs to my bedroom. I grab a couple of the plush white towels and race back to Jake as quickly as I can. He is sat in his office chair and is on the phone talking to someone. I don't ask questions, I just go and wrap the wound as best as I can, with the towels, to try and stop the blood flow. He says, to whoever is on the phone, that he will be waiting outside and then he gets up, walks past me, and heads for the hall way.

"Um, Jake? Where the bloody hell are you going?" I stand with my hands on my hips and wait for him to answer me.

"To the hospital. Eric is on his way to take me." He doesn't even turn around to look at me. I scurry after him. I manage to overtake him in the hall way and I stand in front of him so that he has to stop walking. He looks at me and I can see a range of emotions flicker through his eyes.

"Now just you hang on. Don't think for one minute that I am not coming with you," I say, defiantly.

"You don't need to do that. It's late and Eric will wait for me."

"Jake Waters, I am coming with you whether you like it or not. I will only sit here worrying about whether you are okay otherwise." I fold my arms across my chest and just stand there. There is no way that I am staying here by myself. I prepare for him to try and fob me off, but to my astonishment he doesn't.

"Thank you," is all he says as he offers up a weak smile. I nod my head, turn around and race downstairs to get my shoes on. I help Jake with his shoes once he reaches the bottom of the stairs, and I put a jacket around him. I open the front door and step outside to see that Eric is already waiting on the drive way. Jake takes some door keys off of the hooks by the door and goes to lock the house up. I grab the keys off of him as I point to the limo. He walks off muttering as I lock the door. I catch up to him and follow him into the limo. Jake has now gone pale and is perspiring. I hold his hand, of his uninjured arm, as we make our way to the hospital.

It doesn't take long for Eric to reach the hospital, and together, Eric and I help Jake out of the limo. We get Jake to the reception desk and, the receptionist, instantly gets Jake sat in a wheelchair. A doctor comes racing over a few seconds later and then we are on the move. We head past a few doors before the doctor enters a big spacious room, complete with bed, sofa and television. It is only now that I realise that we are in a private hospital rather than the NHS one. *Of course, he's a millionaire, why would he not pay a fortune for healthcare?* I go to exit the room with Eric when Jake grabs my arm with his good hand.

"Stay with me," he says in a quiet voice. His eyes are pleading with me, but it doesn't take me more than a second to make my decision. I smile and gently shake my arm from his grasp, before taking a seat on the sofa. He smiles at me and the doctor tells Jake to sit on the bed. I remain silent as the doctor examines Jake and says he will need to have some shards of glass removed from his arm, and then he will need a few stitches. Jake lets out a groan as the doctor leaves the room to retrieve the required equipment.

"How are you feeling?" I ask him as I walk over and stand by the side of the bed.

"Scared," Jake answers.

"Scared?"

Jake sighs. "I hate needles." I can't help but giggle at him. "What's so funny?" he raises one eyebrow and looks at me quizzically.

"You mean that a big, strong man like you has a fear of little, tiny needles?" I can't stop laughing.

"Oh, I'm glad you find this so funny," he says. He may not sound too thrilled but I can see his eyes light up as he watches me.

"I'm sorry. I just wasn't expecting you to be scared of something like that."

"It's my only weakness, I swear." He manages a tiny smile but it soon evaporates as he grimaces from the pain in his arm. The doctor returns so I once again take my seat on the sofa. Once the doctor is satisfied that he has removed all of the glass, he then cleans the wound, which I can tell is causing Jake immense pain if his facial expressions and use of foul language are anything to go by. I jump up and go over to hold his good hand. Jake squeezes my hand slightly, which I take to mean as a thank you. The doctor then stitches Jake's arm and bandages the wound.

"You will need to rest Jake. The wound isn't as bad as it looks, but you need to make sure you don't do anything to aggravate the healing process. I will see you in two days' time. I will book you an appointment and forward you the details." The doctor stands up and Jake and I both thank him. He smiles, nods and then exits the room.

"You heard the doc, you have to rest." I reiterate to Jake.

"I don't do resting. I have a company to run." He does not look pleased. Jake doesn't seem like the type of guy to follow orders.

"Well, it's lucky for you that I will be on hand to help then, isn't it?" Jake frowns and I give him a smirk before walking towards the door. "Come on then scaredy cat. Let's get you home and away from any sight of needles."

"Ha ha, very funny." I can hear the amusement in his voice though as he follows me out of the room and out of the hospital to the limo.

Chapter Fourteen.

We arrive back at the house as the early morning workers make their daily commute. I leave Jake to speak to Eric as I go and unlock the front door. I walk straight into the kitchen where I grab Jake a glass of water. I decide to make some toast as well, seeing as neither of us has had anything to eat. Jake appears a few moments later and watches me from the kitchen doorway.

"What?" I ask him.

"Nothing," he replies.

"Well, in that case, get your butt up to bed and I will bring this up to you." I point in the direction of the stairs. Jake stands to attention and salutes me before marching off up the stairs. He really does make me smile. I busy myself getting the toast ready and then I find a tray to carry it all upstairs on. I decide against making any coffee as I am hoping that I will be able to have a little nap. With caffeine in my system, there would be no way I would be able to rest. As I make my way up the stairs, I cast my mind back to the conversation Jake was having with the mysterious Caitlin woman in his office. I just can't understand why Jake spoke to her like that. I am yet to see a bad side to him. I don't want to think badly of him because he has helped me so much in the last couple of days. God, is that all it's been? Two days? It feels like I have been here so much longer with all that has happened so far. I don't know how much more shock I can take. I still haven't really had much time to process the whole Donnie situation, but maybe that's a good thing. Keeping busy is better than dwelling over it. I wish I could call Lydia though. I feel saddened as I think of how she walked out on me, and that I haven't heard from her since. I shake my head as I reach Jake's bedroom. I can think about that another time. Right now, Jake needs my attention. The door to his bedroom is open, but I don't feel comfortable just walking in. I can see Jake's bed which is even bigger than the one that I have been sleeping in. How is that even possible? I spot a sofa which runs along the length of the window on the back wall. The décor is very simple. Cream walls and black furnishings. Very manly. Jake comes into view, emerging from a doorway in his room, and strides across his bedroom. He is wearing just a black pair of silk boxer shorts. My god, he is just perfection. I admire his physique as he sits on the bed and looks at me standing in the doorway.

"Are you coming in?" He asks, a smirk visible on his lips.

"Uh, I didn't feel right just walking in without asking," I say, feeling stupid. I start shuffling on the spot due to nerves creeping in at the thought of going into Jake's bedroom.

"Don't be silly. You're welcome in my bedroom any time," he winks at me. I feel myself swoon. *Get a bloody grip Stacey,* I tell myself. *The guy has just come home from the hospital. He is your friend and nothing more.* I casually stroll over to the bed and put the toast, and glass of water, on his bedside table. I motion for Jake to get into his bed and lie down. He does so and I turn and walk from the room without saying a word. I quickly go to my bedroom across the hall and retrieve the soft blanket that lies across the end of my bed, and a pillow. I go back to Jake's room and head for the sofa.

"Stace," Jake says my name to get my attention. "What are you doing?" He looks puzzled as I put the pillow on the sofa and get myself settled under the blanket. I sink into the sofa, and my body is instantly grateful for the pure softness that is enveloping my body. I stifle a groan at how comfortable it is.

"What does it look like I'm doing?" I answer sarcastically. He remains silent and I grin. "I am staying in here with you just in case you need anything. Is that a problem Mr Waters?"

"There really is no need. I haven't lost a limb. I've just cut my arm."

"Don't argue with me because you won't win. Now, eat your toast and then get some rest. I don't know about you, but after the events of the last few days, I'm exhausted." Forgetting about needing to eat any toast myself, I close my eyes and hope that he will take the hint. I hear Jake chuckle to himself as I curl up on my side and get some much-needed rest.

Chapter Fifteen.

I am awoken by the sound of banging downstairs. I groggily look over to Jake's bed, but he is fast asleep. *That's weird. Maybe it's Eric?* Whoever it is, they are making quite a racket for me to be able to hear it up here on the third floor. I drag my body off of the sofa and head downstairs to see what all the noise is about. As I get closer to the ground floor, it appears that the noise is coming from the kitchen. I walk along the ground floor hall way and enter the kitchen to see a blonde-haired woman banging pots around. The kitchen is an absolute mess, with food and crockery scattered everywhere. *What the fuck is going on?* The woman has her back to me so it isn't until I speak that she realises that I am here.

"What the hell are you doing?" I ask the strange woman. She spins around and fixes me with a deadly stare. Her dark brown eyes burn into me and make me feel uncomfortable. Her face is screwed up and she looks pissed off. I can only assume that she is annoyed at my unexpected interruption.

"I'm cooking. What the fuck has it got to do with you?" she snarls at me. Thank goodness that she is on the other side of the kitchen island, because she looks positively evil. I stay in the kitchen doorway to keep my distance from her. For all I know this woman is a complete psycho.

"Um, should you be here?" I am more than confused as to what is going on.

"Of course I should. I am making Jake a meal. Who the hell are you and what are you doing here?" The venom in her voice is obvious. This woman lacks some serious manners.

"I don't think that's important, but I do think that you should leave," I say, firmly. I start to feel extremely wary around her.

"I'm not going anywhere." And just like that, it appears that we are in a stand-off. I really don't have the energy for all of this. So much for all the shocks being over and done with.

"Jake needs to rest, and he isn't up to visitors at the moment. Why don't you come back another time?" A change of tactic may work. At least I am hoping that it will.

"Who are you?" she asks again, her eyebrows draw together and her eyes narrow.

I sigh. "I'm a friend of Jake's. I'm looking after him seeing as he has had a bit of an accident."

She scoffs. "Accident? Is that what he told you?" *Ah, the penny drops. This must be Caitlin. Oh Christ, that's all I need to deal with, Jake's scorned ex.*

"There is no reason for him to lie to me." Of course I am not going to admit to her that Jake has tried to pass off the vase incident as a mere case of his own clumsiness. Caitlin smirks.

"You're one of those tramps he likes to screw, aren't you?" I am gobsmacked at her question. Before I can form words to answer her, she continues to speak. "For your information, Jake did not have an accident. He was going to throw the vase at me, so I grabbed it off of him and hit his arm with it." My mind processes her words. Surely this woman isn't telling the truth? From what I know of Jake, I am certain that he wouldn't physically hurt any woman. Then again, maybe I am a poor judge of character? She watches for my reaction. I don't know how I manage it, but I don't move an inch, not even a facial twitch. "Why don't you run along home and I will continue to tend to Jake's needs." Ugh, this woman is repulsive. I am way too tired to deal with this bullshit, so I decide to play her at her own game.

"Listen here Caitlin." Her eyes go wide as I say her name. "I think you need to get the fuck out of this house before this situation gets out of hand. Jake has told me all about you, and you are not welcome here. If you don't leave then I will be forced to call the police, which I'm sure is the last thing you want." Caitlin just stares at me, but I never break away from her gaze. After a few long, tense minutes, it seems that she has come to her senses as she grabs her bag and walks towards me. I step back to let her pass. She stops, inches from me, and looks me up and down. I feel my defences rise at her sinister stare. Adrenaline pumps through my system as I realise that this situation could get more heated than it is already. After an unbearably awkward few seconds, she simply smirks, shakes her head, turns away and starts walking to the front door. She opens the front door and stops, still with her back to me.

"Don't think that this is the last you will be hearing from me bitch." My heart hammers against my chest as she slams the door behind her. I run to it and lock it. I lean my back against the door as I take a few deep breaths. *Fuck, she was rather scary.* In one way I am proud that I stood up to her, but in another way I think how stupid I was to confront her. I shakily walk back to the kitchen, feeling deflated, as I look at all of the mess she has made. I better clean all of this up before Jake sees it. At least doing this will keep my mind occupied for a while. My life really has become bizarre over the past few days. And now, with this Caitlin issue, it seems that there is more to Mr Waters than meets the eye. I spend the next half an hour chucking the food Caitlin was making into the bin, and washing everything that she appears to have touched. I am half way through the mess when Jake enters the kitchen.

"Having a Gordon Ramsey moment are we?" he asks, unaware of the conflict that happened in here not so long ago.

"I wasn't, but some woman called Caitlin was." I wait and watch his reaction. He visibly recoils at the mention of her name. I decide now is the time to ask about her, before he has the chance to change the topic. "Who is she Jake?"

"She's not important." His jaw clenches as he looks at his arm.

"Are we really going to do this?" I ask.

"Do what?"

"Skirt around the subject. I know that she was here last night and I know her version of events, so why not just tell me your side of the story?" It may not be my place, but if I am staying here, then I need to know the truth. Jake runs his hands through his hair and takes a seat at the kitchen island.

"I need scotch for a conversation like this, but seeing as I'm on medication, would you mind making me a coffee?" he asks. I turn and pick up one of the clean cups off of the draining board, and make Jake his coffee. I make one for myself at the same time, seeing as I haven't had chance to beforehand. I walk around the kitchen island and sit on the stool next to Jake. Jake sips his coffee and I wait patiently for him to start talking. After what feels like an eternity, he finally starts to speak. "I have known Caitlin for three years. She came to work for me as my PA. She had been working with me for over two years, when I stupidly decided to mix business with pleasure. I slept with her, on and off, for a few months, but I was never in a relationship with her. I suppose you could say that I led her to believe that we were a couple because, to be honest, I never told her otherwise." I say nothing as I want to hear where he is going with this. "I stopped sleeping with her after I spent the night with you, six months ago. I just couldn't do it anymore. It felt wrong after being with you." Well, knock me down with a feather, I wasn't expecting that. I decide not to comment as I don't really want to bring attention to the fact that we had a one night stand together. Especially as we are starting to form a friendship. "She took it well at first, but things soon changed. She became erratic and wouldn't leave me alone. I had to fire her as my PA as she kept messing up my meetings and making me look bad. After I fired her, she said that she was pregnant." I gasp at this piece of news as it comes as a shock. Jake puts his head in his hands. "I didn't want to have a child with her, but I thought that I should step up and take responsibility for my actions. It was coming up to the first scan and I had arranged to meet her at the hospital. Only, she wasn't at the hospital when I got there, and with a bit of persuasion, I found out that they didn't even have her on their records. She lied about the pregnancy. She believed that I wouldn't turn up to the scan, and she thought that she would get away with the lie for a bit longer. I then told her I wanted nothing more to do with her, but her behaviour just keeps getting more and more crazy. She tries to follow my every move. Then last night, she showed up here as you are already aware. She got angry with me, and that's when she smashed the vase and cut my arm." I sit there and take in everything that he has just told me. My gut feeling tells me to trust him, and to trust what he is saying.

"So, what you're saying is, on top of everything else going on, I now have to worry about some lunatic ex of yours that now knows I am staying here? Wow, this has been quite a week, and it's not even over with yet." My life has turned into some kind of soap opera.

"I'm sorry, but I didn't think you would ever have the misfortune of meeting her."

"I understand why you never said anything. I mean, I've only been here a few days, why the hell would you tell me? We still hardly know each other. I will say though, if I am going to be staying here until I get myself sorted, then you need to update me on things like this. It would be nice to have a heads up. That way, at least I can try and prepare myself for altercations like the one I had with her an hour ago."

"I'm sorry," Jake looks genuinely apologetic, then his face suddenly lights up. "Did I just hear you say that you are going to stay here?" His eyebrows are raised in anticipation. It seems like he really does want me to stay here.

"Yes Jake. Who else is going to look after you? Besides Caitlin of course," I smile at my comment. I need to try and make the best of this situation.

"Not funny Stace."

"Sorry, just trying to lighten the mood." I get up from the stool and continue with tidying the kitchen.

"Are you really okay with what I just told you?" Jake seems surprised.

"Hey, it could be worse. So you have a psycho ex, big deal. Everyone has baggage." I shrug my shoulders as I put the last of the pans away. "Besides, life is full of struggles, it's just how you deal with them that matters." I lean on the island and look into Jake's eyes. Something passes between us, but I can't pin point what it is.

"You're incredible you know that?" I feel myself blush at Jake's words, but I just want to keep the mood light.

"I do try," I tease. "How about I cook us some food and you can go and pick out a movie for us to watch?" In my opinion, there are no other words needed on the Caitlin matter. He has told me all that I need to know, and for that I am grateful. It just shows that he must trust me enough for him to tell me. I hear Jake's stomach grumble at the mention of food.

"That would be great," he says. I smile at him and I take pleasure in being able to look after him. He gets up from the stool and is about to exit the kitchen when a question pops into my head.

"Just one more thing," I say. Jake turns around and looks at me. "How did she even get in here? Does she have a key?" *Oh god, please don't say she has a bloody key*. Jake sighs and looks just as confused as I must do.

"No, she most certainly does not have a key. I can only think that I must have forgotten to lock the patio doors last night."

"Hmmm. Maybe we need to be more vigilant about locking doors from now on then?"

"Agreed."

"Don't worry, I locked the front door when she left. I will go and lock the patio doors whilst you go and put your feet up."

"Yes ma'am," Jake replies in a cocky manner. He salutes and I laugh at his playfulness. I shoo him away and am overcome with a sense that, just maybe, I was meant to meet Jake for a reason. He really does seem to have a way of making me feel at ease, even with all the crazy going on around me. Psycho ex's aside, I feel very lucky to have had the fortune of meeting him. My perfect stranger, most certainly, is keeping me on my toes.

Chapter Sixteen.

"I am so full," I whine as my stomach hurts from eating too much food.

"That was delicious," Jake says as he lies back on the sofa. I cooked us an Indian feast which, I have to agree, was very tasty. I ask Jake to pause the film as I get up and take all of the plates and dishes into the kitchen. I pile them all on the side as I don't have the inclination to even place them in the dishwasher right now. There are some left over samosa's and onion bahji's, so I find a container to put them in and I place them in the fridge. I pour myself a glass of wine from the bottle that Jake opened for me to have with my food, and I head back to the lounge. Jake is on soft drinks due to the medication he is taking for the pain in his arm.

"You know Jake," I start to say as I sit down next to him and cover myself with the blanket he is hogging. "I don't think you could have picked a more inappropriate film than this."

"What do you mean? It's a good thriller."

"You choose Gone Girl and yet we have had your crazy ex here twice in the last twenty-four hours. Are you missing her already?" I tease him. The irony is uncanny. I also think that the wine is making me a little bit more loose lipped than I normally am.

"Oh god Stace, please don't joke about that." He's pulling the most ridiculous faces at the thought. I laugh hysterically.

"If someone had told me last week that all these different things were going to happen to me, then I would have thought that they were on drugs."

"I know. It's been a bit of a rollercoaster," Jake replies. I place my wine glass on the coffee table and turn to look at him. I need him to know how much I appreciate what he has done for me, and I feel now is the time to say it.

"Jake, I am so grateful to you for helping me in The Den the other night. You will never know how relieved I was to see you standing there. And I just wanted to say that what you have done for me since then is more than I deserve. I am indebted to you, and I will pay you back one day, somehow. I'm just not sure how yet." Tears prick the backs of my eyes. "I haven't had anyone look after me this way in such a long time. I have no family left, and it's nice to feel protected by someone. I'm really glad that I can class you as a friend." Jake's gaze penetrates into my eyes. I now feel a little bit silly for being so open with him, but I needed him to know. Jake cups my cheek with his good hand.

"It's no problem. It's nice to have someone to look after." It is taking all of my willpower not to lean in and kiss him. My body is humming with need for him, but I can't let myself give in. I clear my throat and excuse myself to go to the bathroom. I choose to run upstairs and use the one in my bedroom, just to get some space. The moment we just shared was intense. I don't want to lose Jake as a friend by doing something stupid. I pace up and down the bathroom, trying to push away all of the emotions that I am feeling. This would be the point where I would phone Lydia and she would probably tell me to stop acting like a muppet and enjoy myself. I miss her. I go to the sink and splash some water on my face. It's in this moment that it suddenly dawns on me that I don't have my phone with me. *Shit, I can't believe that I have gone all this time with no phone and I have only just realised.* And I haven't thought about my laptop either. Mind you, with everything that's been going on, I'm surprised that I even remember my own name. I dry my face as there is a knock on the bathroom door.

"Stace, is everything okay?" Jake says, concern etched in his tone of voice. *Come on Stace. Don't let him see that he is affecting you. He's just your friend.*

"Yeah I'm fine. I'll be out in a minute." I give myself a check in the mirror. My cheeks are a little flushed but apart from that, I look okay. I open the bathroom door and Jake is standing there, looking like some sort of God. He may only be wearing jogging bottoms and a t-shirt, but my oh my, he looks good enough to devour. I watch him as he rakes his eyes over my body. I may only be wearing some leggings and an oversized shirt, but Jake manages to make me feel as sexy as hell from his gaze. The heat that emanates from him nearly floors me. I take in a deep breath and am about to ask him to kindly move out of the way, when he surges towards me, grabs me at my waist and places his lips on mine. He picks me up and I automatically wrap my legs around his waist and our kiss becomes more desperate. He walks us towards the sink unit and sits me on top of the counter. I keep my legs wrapped around him, enjoying the feel of his body so close. As the urgency of our kiss continues, I run my hands through his hair and hear him let out a quiet moan. What this man does to me is remarkable. The electricity between us is so powerful, it's almost frightening. Jake continues to explore my mouth with his tongue as his hands tighten their grip on my waist. My sex is already wet with my need for him. I move my hands to the bottom of his t-shirt and lift the hem slightly so that I can feel his skin beneath my fingertips when Jake abruptly stops the kissing and touching. My legs break from around his waist as he backs away from me with wide eyes. I frantically search his face for answers, but I find none. We are both breathing heavy and the sound is deafening in the otherwise silent room. It's almost as if Jake's shutters have come down and he has blocked out all emotions.

"I can't do this." Those are the only words he speaks as I look at him, dumbfounded. I watch as he practically runs from the bathroom. I sit, shell shocked, on the sink. *What the hell just happened? Why did he leave? Did I do something wrong? Am I a bad kisser?* I have a million different questions going around in my head, and I have no answers to any of them. I suddenly feel raw and exposed. It is a stark contrast to the heat and passion I felt only seconds ago. My body reacts to the rejection. I feel cold and unwanted, not to mention stupid. I shouldn't have let him kiss me. I shouldn't have given in to my urges. Now, the friendship Jake and I were building, has been shattered into a million pieces. We have just begun getting to know each other, and now its ruined. The hurt that I am feeling right now is indescribable. Pain sears through me as hopes for Jake to be a part of my life have been dashed.

Chapter Seventeen.

I am barely aware of what I am doing until I am half way down the road and walking in the direction of Lydia's flat. I know we left things on bad terms but I need to see her right now. I hope we can put aside our differences. I really need to talk to her, and I really need to be away from Jake. I don't know where he went after the bathroom incident, but I didn't see him again. It starts to rain and all I have on is the same clothes that I left the house in. I didn't even think to grab a jacket. All I thought about was getting my shoes on and getting the hell out of there. Marvellous, I now get to look like a drowned rat as I walk along the pavement. I fold my arms across my chest and quicken my walking pace. It only takes me twenty minutes and I am stood in front of Lydia's front door. It's late so I hope that she is still awake. I summon up all of my courage and I knock on her door. It takes a few moments but eventually Lydia answers the door. She gasps as she sees me.

"Hi," I say shyly. I don't know what else to say. I would normally just walk in, but I wait to see if she invites me in this time.

"Uh, hi. I wasn't expecting to see you?" Lydia asks a question rather than just making a statement.

"I just um, I just…….." *I just what? Got rejected by the guy that I am developing feelings for? How pathetic would that sound?* I search for words but nothing comes. Instead I just stand there looking at the floor, feeling like an utter fool.

"You better come in. You must be freezing." Lydia ushers me inside. "Let me go and grab you a towel. Your clothes are still in the spare bedroom if you want to go and get changed."

"Oh. Thanks Lyd," I gratefully smile at her. She goes off to get me a towel and I head to the spare bedroom. I don't fail to notice that Lydia didn't refer to it as my room, so I'm guessing that she is still angry with me. I enter the room and everything is exactly as I left it a few days ago, nothing has been moved. Lydia comes back with a towel and says that she will go and make us a hot drink. I quickly dry myself and get changed into some jogging bottoms and a black jumper. I look at my phone, which is still on the bedside table. I pick it up and try to turn it on to see if anyone has called, but there is no charge left in it. Bloody typical! Now I can't see if anyone has tried to contact me. I place the phone in the pocket of my jogging bottoms. I will just have to check for any messages another time. I go through to the lounge where Lydia is sitting on the sofa with a mug of hot chocolate in her hands. She points to my mug on the coffee table. I feel awkward, something that I have never felt in Lydia's presence before. She gestures for me to sit down next to her. I oblige and pick up my mug. I take a sip and am grateful for the warm chocolate that heats my insides.

"So, how have you been?" I ask her. I figure this is the best way to try and break the tension between us.

"Not great actually." Her reply is solemn. Silence engulfs the room and makes it feel smaller somehow. Shit,

I should have thought of something else to ask. I mentally curse myself for making things seem more uncomfortable.

"Listen Lyd........" I am cut off before I can continue.

"No. I need to talk first." Lydia holds her hands up as she speaks. I purse my lips together and dread what she may be about to say. "I'm sorry that I ran out and left you the other day. I just wasn't expecting to be told something like that. I needed to be on my own and just think things through. I guess it was the shock that made me react like that. When I came back here, I found Donnie sitting in the kitchen drinking a cup of coffee. His face was a mess. He acted like nothing was wrong to start with. Anyway, I tricked him to see if he would tell me the truth, but he didn't." Lydia takes a deep breath and pushes her hair away from her face. "Deep down, I knew that you would never lie about something like that. I knew that I had made a huge mistake by ever letting him into my life. As he was talking, he made my skin crawl. After he gave some piss poor excuse about being attacked by some random group of men, I let him have it. I shouted at him until I could shout no more. Not for what he has done to me, but for what he has put you through." Lydia takes a pause and I can see her eyes glaze over. I feel utter relief wash over me that Lydia believes me. "I told him that I never wanted to see him again, and if I ever did, then I would tell everyone about what he had done. I also said I would tell everyone the fact that he had a small penis, just for good measure." I feel a smile pull at my lips when she says the last bit. "I have been trying to call you ever since that day, but your phone has just been going to voicemail. I thought that you didn't want to talk to me."

"Oh god, that's not the case at all." I pull my phone out of my pocket and show her that it has no battery. "I left the phone here Lyd. It's been in the spare bedroom the whole time. That's why I never got your calls."

"Oh. So, do you forgive me?" Lydia asks tentatively.

"There is nothing to forgive you for. I'm just glad that Donnie hasn't come between us." With that, we both stand up and give each other a hug. Tears start to fall down my cheeks as I feel a piece of my life slot back into place. Thank goodness for that. I really thought that we weren't going to be able to patch things up. Lydia pulls away first and wipes tears from her own face.

"Now, enough of this crying lark. We have wasted too much time talking about that asshole Donnie already. What we should be talking about is that hunk of man that you have been staying with." I am so glad that Lydia doesn't want to talk about Donnie anymore. He is the last person I want to be thinking about. However, the subject of Jake isn't exactly a happy one at the moment either.

"Oh Lyd, it's all such a mess." New tears emerge, only this time they are laced with sadness rather than joy.

"Oh fuck. Start from the beginning," Lydia says. "We have all night if needs be. I'm not at work tomorrow and, of course, you can stay here. That's if you want to?" She seems unsure about whether I will or not.

"That would be great. Thank you." She smiles at me and I get myself comfortable on the sofa as I proceed to explain to Lydia about all the events that have happened over the last few days. Lydia listens patiently as I pour my heart out to her. I can't shake off the sense of feeling naïve and stupid. I shouldn't have let my guard down with Jake. I knew that he was too good to be true. When Caitlin showed up, I should have just got the hell out of there. I can see that Lydia wants to give her honest opinion, but when I look at the clock it says that it is three in the morning. Where did the time go? I feel exhausted, so we both decide to pick up this conversation again when we have got some much needed rest. I give Lydia a hug goodnight before plodding to the spare bedroom. I daren't call it my bedroom again yet, just in case something else happens to kick me in the teeth. I keep my jogging bottoms and jumper on, and I climb into bed. As soon as my head hits the pillow, sleep consumes me.

Chapter Eighteen.

I wake up to the sound of Lydia crashing into the spare bedroom. I jolt upright in bed and look over to see that she has fallen over and landed on her ass. I break out into a fit of laughter at the sight of her. I have missed her antics over the last few days.

"Shit Stace. He's here! He's here!" she says, breathlessly.

"Who's here?" I ask, the laughter dying on my lips as I start to panic that Donnie has shown up. The fear in my voice is evident, and my heart starts to beat a little faster.

"Jake!"

"WHAT?" I shout.

"Sssshhhh, he will hear you."

"Lyd, I'm pretty sure that the entire block heard you fall over just now." I smile at her. I also experience a flutter in my stomach at the thought of Jake being near.

"He's standing outside the front door. Do you want to see him?" she enquires. I ponder her question for a few moments. One half of me would love to see him, but the other half of me is still hurt by his rejection. I need to remain sensible in my choice.

"No. I don't want to see him. If he asks, just tell him that you haven't seen me." I need to stay strong, for my own sake more than anything.

"No worries babes. Lydia to the rescue." She hops to her feet and bounds out of the bedroom, shutting the door behind her on the way. I feel nerves start to kick in and the butterflies are dancing around frantically inside me. I feel my body hum as I know that he is near. I daren't move from the bed for fear of making noise. He can't know that I am here. I stay sat in my upright position as I listen to their muffled voices. I am dying for the toilet but I desperately hold it in. After ten minutes, I hear the front door shut and Lydia comes back into the spare bedroom. She takes a seat at the end of the bed. I look at her, waiting for her to speak. After a few seconds she still hasn't spoken and I can be patient no longer.

"Well?" I ask her.

"He came to apologise for his behaviour. I don't think he believed me when I said that I hadn't seen you. He asked if he could take you to dinner, to explain things to you."

"Like hell am I going to dinner with him!" I can't believe the nerve of the guy. *Does he think that by taking me for some fancy dinner that it will soften the blow of his rejection? Not bloody likely!*

"He did look really sorry Stace. He doesn't look like he has slept either. Even so, he still looks dangerously fuckable." Lydia has a dreamy look on her face and I can't help but laugh at her. "Maybe you should talk to him and tell him how you really feel?"

"No. I don't want to," I sigh. I will have to face him at some point, considering that he has the majority of my possessions at his house. I'm just not ready to face him today. "There is no way that I am telling that man anything. I need to forget about Jake Waters. Actually, I need to just forget about men full stop for a while. Plus, I want to spend the day chilling with my bestie. What do you say? Wine and chick flicks?"

"Sounds like a plan to me. What a gripping life we do lead," Lydia says whilst she gives me a cynical look. I know that I am not fooling her with saying that I need to forget about Jake, but I am trying my hardest to.

"Hey, I will take boring and predictable over the last few days any time."

"I think on this occasion I have to agree with you. I will nip out and get some wine, and I'll pick up some nibbles too." Lydia stands and goes to walk out of the room but she pauses at the door and turns back to face me. "Just promise me that you will think about speaking to Jake. I know you don't want to do it right now, but you might change your mind in a few days. He seems genuine." She then bounces out of the room before I can reply. I choose to ignore what she just said. I need to focus on myself for a bit. I get out of bed and go to the bathroom to relieve myself now that Jake has gone. Lydia calls out that she is leaving and that she will be back as quick as possible. I finish up in the bathroom and go to the kitchen to put the kettle on. Whilst waiting for the kettle I go back to the spare bedroom to find my phone charger, only to find Jake sat on the end of the bed. I give a high-pitched shriek at the shock of him being in here. My heart is racing and it takes all my energy to try and remain calm.

"What the hell are you doing here?" My shock is quickly overtaken by anger. He looks at me with dark bags under his eyes. Lydia was right, he doesn't look like he has slept. I have to agree with her on the still looking dangerously fuckable part too. I push any sexual thoughts out of my mind so as not to cloud my judgement. "How dare you barge in here. Who do you think you are?" Jake may not be the kind of guy to take orders from people, but actually entering a property without permission is pushing the boundaries ever so slightly.

"Stacey, I came to say that I am sorry for how I handled things last night. It was wrong of me to push you away like that. I can't imagine how you must have felt."

"You can't? Well, let me give you a hint shall I? Hurt, confused, rejected, do I need to go on?" I am so angry. How dare he invade my space and privacy like this.

"No, I get it. I didn't want to hurt you. I wanted to explain stuff to you over dinner, but a part of me knew that you wouldn't agree to that. I knew that Lydia was covering for you by saying that she hadn't seen you. I had to find a way of speaking to you Stace." He sounds desperate, but in my irate state I couldn't care less.

"So you just come in here uninvited? Do you respect anyone's privacy Jake?"

"Of course I do, but like I said, I needed to speak to you."

"I don't want to hear what you have to say." I'm being stubborn. Of course I want to hear what he has to say, but I don't want to make it easy for him.

"In that case, I think that it's best that you don't stay with me anymore." His tone turns cold and flat. I wasn't expecting that to be his next line at all. Anger flares up within me again.

"Oh you don't? And I suppose you thought that by taking me to dinner that you would have done your best to break this news to me gently?" Sarcasm drips from my voice. "Well, let me make this easy for you. I wouldn't come back to yours if you paid me. I will collect my stuff as soon as possible." I can hear myself speaking and I don't like what I hear. This isn't me. This is just pent up anger over this whole situation.

"It's okay. I'll have all your stuff sent over here for you. There's no need for you to come to the house." He doesn't look at me as he speaks. If I thought that I couldn't hurt anymore, I was wrong. It is like a stabbing to my heart. What did I do to make him behave this way towards me? Maybe his psycho ex *was* right about how things went down with them the other night? Maybe he is the one who is lying?

"Fine. Now, please will you leave. I have nothing more to say to you." I look away from him and stare out of the window. I can't bear to watch him walk out of here knowing that I won't see or speak to him again. I hear him stand and walk to the bedroom door.

"Goodbye Stacey," are his final words to me. I don't answer him. I couldn't answer him even if I wanted to. My throat feels like it has closed up. My life just keeps going wrong. I don't understand what I did to deserve this. I feel my heart breaking, but I don't understand why it hurts so much.

Chapter Nineteen.

Lydia comes back to find me curled up on the sofa with my duvet wrapped around me, and used tissues strewn about the place.

"Christ Stace, what happened to you? I wasn't gone that long was I?"

"I saw Jake," I say sadly as more tears threaten to emerge.

"I'll go open the wine," Lydia says and she goes into the kitchen without saying another word. All I seem to have done this week is cry. I'm surprised that I have any tears left. Lydia returns with two large glasses of rose wine, and makes me sit up so that she can sit next to me. Lydia gets snuggled under my quilt with her wine and I inform her of what happened when I found Jake in the bedroom. There isn't much to tell though so it doesn't take long for me to relay it all to her.

"Shit. I thought he had left when I said you weren't here. I thought I was convincing. There was no sign of him when I went out. The sneaky sod must have been waiting along the corridor," she says, almost as if she is just clarifying her own thoughts out loud.

"Why do I feel like this Lyd? I've never had feelings like this before, not even with Charles in our earlier days." I am desperate for answers, but nothing is coming to me. Whatever the reason is for me feeling like this, I sure as hell don't like it, and I don't know how to deal with it.

"Far be it for me to point out the obvious Stace but, I think you have developed feelings for this guy that are a lot stronger than you may have realised."

"Don't be ridiculous. I've only known him for a few days."

"So? Who's to say how long it takes to fall for someone. It can happen in an instant." Lydia, ever the romantic even after her failed relationships. I think about what she says, but I can't admit to myself just how much I like him. I drain my wine glass and get up off of the sofa to go and pour myself another one. The doorbell rings whilst I am mid-pour. I put the wine bottle down with a sigh and I go to answer the door. Surely nothing else can go wrong today? I open the door to find two men standing there. I have never seen these guys before in my life.

"Stacey Paris?" The tall, bald one asks me. He looks rather menacing and I feel the hairs on the back of my neck prickle.

"Uh, yeah, that's me." My eyes turn to look at the shorter man. He is far stockier than the tall one, but looks just as hard faced. *Who the hell are these guys? And how do they know my name?*

"We have your belongings from Mr Waters. We will start to bring the stuff up." Neither of them says anything else. Turning around, they head back down the stairs to, I presume, get all of my belongings. These guys certainly get to the point quickly. And Jake certainly isn't wasting any time in making sure that I am out of his life. Lydia appears in the lounge doorway, breaking me from my thoughts.

"Who is it now? It's like Piccadilly Circus in here today," Lydia exclaims.

"It's my stuff from Jake's. Some guys are dropping it off."

"Seriously?" She looks just as flabbergasted as I feel. "Ugh, what an asshole. He didn't hang around did he?" Lydia's words near enough echo my thoughts from a moment ago.

"Better to get it done and out of the way I suppose," I say to her with a shrug of my shoulders. If Jake doesn't want me in his life, then that's his loss. The two guys return, carrying a large box each. I direct them to the spare bedroom and tell them to pile as much in there as they possibly can. Of course the bedroom won't be big enough for everything, so Lydia says that the rest can go in her bedroom for now. Thank goodness we made up, because I have no idea where I would be right now otherwise. It doesn't take long for the meaty looking men to bring my stuff up. When they have finished, I thank them and close the door as they leave. "More wine Lydia. I've got a lot of sorting out to do."

"I'm on it babes." Lydia disappears into the kitchen. I survey the boxes before me. My whole life is packed into them. What a truly pathetic sight it is. I start going through the boxes in my room first, so that I can make room for the ones that are residing in Lydia's bedroom. Most of the boxes are full of clothes. I start making three piles. One for charity, one for the rubbish bin, and one for the stuff that I am going to keep. I am halfway through the first box when

Lydia returns with the wine. I gratefully take my glass off of her and take a long sip. She watches me for a few moments before she speaks.

"Hey, why don't you come to The Den with me tomorrow daytime? We could sort out some shifts for you?" To say that I am surprised at her suggestion is an understatement. I almost spit my mouthful of wine at her.

"I don't know Lyd. The Den doesn't exactly hold the greatest of memories for me at this moment in time." I shudder as a picture of Donnie forms in my mind. I shake my head to try and rid myself of the image.

"I know that, but it would be nice to have you working with me again. The offer is still there." Lydia smiles affectionately. "Plus, you shouldn't let that low life bastard Donnie stop you from going somewhere that you love to go. The security team know never to let him in again too, so he would have to be a miracle worker to get in." At least Lydia understands why I am reluctant to return there. I know that she is trying to help, but I need to be confident enough to return to The Den. And right now, I don't feel confident at all. I need to shut down Lydia's attempts at trying to get me to go there though, without dismissing the idea completely.

"I will seriously think about it. I just need a bit more time. Thanks though Lyd. I do appreciate the offer." It's all I can say to keep her suggestions to a minimum. Once Lydia forms an idea in her head, there is no stopping her until she has achieved the result that she wants.

"It's the least I can do." Lydia then starts to help me unpack the boxes and sort each item into their relevant pile. There is no more talk of The Den, which I am relieved about. It takes us a couple of hours to clear all of the boxes. We have even managed to sort the ones in Lydia's room too. During the unpacking process, we have managed to polish off the remainder of the bottle of wine, and we are just starting a second bottle. I stand in the bedroom doorway and look at all of our hard work. *My* bedroom may look a little cluttered, but at least I have all of my stuff here. I'm feeling brave enough to consider it my bedroom again now. I don't think Lydia will be kicking me out. I was stupid to think that she would do that in the first place. Shock can do crazy things to your mind. I decide that I will get rid of all the rubbish tomorrow and then I will take the other stuff to the charity shop. All the unwanted items are currently lining the hall way, so I need to get rid of it all as soon as possible. At least that will give me something to do tomorrow. I decide to have an early night as I am physically and mentally exhausted. I'm sure that the wine has helped me to feel even more tired. I say goodnight to Lydia and drag my weary body to my bedroom. As I get into bed, I realise that I still haven't switched my phone on. I get back out of bed with a groan to locate my phone charger. After a few minutes I find the charger underneath my bed. It must have got shoved there during the sorting out process. I plug the charger in to the plug socket by the bedside table and then attach my phone. After a few minutes, there is enough charge in the phone for me to be able to turn it on, whilst it is still charging. I settle back into bed and wait to see what messages are going to come through. I have a few missed calls from Lydia, which I can see are the ones I missed whilst I was staying at Jake's. I also have a text from Susie, a text from Martin, ten missed calls from Charles and a couple of messages from him too. I open Susie's message first. She is just texting to see how I am. I tap out a quick reply to her and then proceed to open Martin's message. He wants to catch up over coffee, which I am more than happy to do. I have missed his infectious personality. I then open the first of Charles' messages. The first one, and the following three, all consist of him grovelling to save himself from embarrassment. I roll my eyes at each one. The final message from him however, really makes me take notice, and pisses me off immensely.

Stacey. I now understand that you probably

don't want to speak to me. I have taken the

liberty of having your car impounded as it was

a nuisance. I apologise but I needed the space.

Regards, Charles.

Oh great. That's just what I needed. An impounded car. Fucking fantastic! The message was sent two days ago, so there will already be costs racking up from the impound lot. He really is such a selfish moron. He has done this out of spite because I won't go back to him. How I ever stayed with him for so long, I really don't know. Although, if I had just have stayed with Charles, none of the events of the last few days would have occurred. Maybe this is all karma for me cheating on Charles all those months ago? I resist the urge to text back a shitty reply. I don't need to stoop to his level, and I definitely don't need to give him the satisfaction of knowing that he has pissed me off. I need to be the bigger person here. I put my phone on the bedside table and lie down. I just stare at the ceiling and try to keep calm. I decide that as of tomorrow, I need to take charge of my life, and sort myself out once and for all.

Chapter Twenty.

I am up and dressed before Lydia even emerges from her bedroom. I have had enough of being made to feel like shit. Today is a new day, and I am going to take charge. Luckily, I have no hangover, which is surprising with the amount of wine I drank last night. I make myself a cup of coffee and take it through to the lounge. I sit on the sofa and put the morning news on, although it is more for background noise than for me to watch. In my mind, I have my whole day planned out. Firstly, I will go and get my car from the impound lot. Secondly, I will use my car to take all of the rubbish to the tip. And thirdly, I will take the rest to the charity shop. The fourth and final thing on my list to do is the most nerve wracking, as it involves going to The Den. Lydia is right. I shouldn't let what happened with Donnie stop me from going there. So, on that basis, I will meet Lydia back here to go with her, when I have finished everything else on my to do list. I need to get back to being strong and independent, and I can't do that if I am living in fear. Lydia walks into the lounge, just as I am finishing my coffee, and flops down next to me on the sofa.

"What are you doing up so early?" she asks me, whilst still yawning. "Are you feeling okay after yesterday?" she looks a little concerned at my complete turnaround.

"I'm fine Lyd. I need to stop wallowing and make stuff happen." I stand up and take my cup into the kitchen. I go to my bedroom, grab my handbag and return to the lounge. "What time are you going to The Den?" I ask Lydia.

"About eleven-ish. Why?"

"I will be back before you leave. Bye Lyd." I don't give her chance to ask any more questions as I turn and head for the front door so that I can start walking to the impound lot. It takes me a while to get there, but I enjoy the peace. It's a relief not to have to discuss Jake with Lydia. When I arrive at the impound lot, I go to a little port-a-cabin that is situated in front of two big steel gates. An old man is sat in there, and he looks bored shitless. He sees me approaching and makes himself look busy.

"Hi," I say. "My car was brought here the other day and I would like to pick it up please." The old man then asks me some details about which car and I tell him all of the necessary information. He taps the information into a computer and then goes to a cupboard, on the back wall, and selects the relevant keys for my car.

"That will be four hundred and fifty pounds to pay." The old guy doesn't bat an eyelid at the amount of money that he has asked me for.

"WHAT?!" I bellow at him.

"Four hundred and fifty pounds. That's the price to get your car back."

"But, how is it so much money?" I am astounded that it could cost this much.

"Two hundred and fifty pounds' collection fee and then one hundred pounds per day for keeping it here." He remains unfazed. He must have to deal with people asking him this question all of the time.

"That's outrageous." The words are out of my mouth before I can stop them. Charles is such a prick. If he thinks that making me pay hundreds of pounds to get my car back is going to make me go back to him, then he is sadly mistaken. I bet in his small mind, he thinks that I am going to ask him to bail me out. No fucking chance. With determination to outwit Charles, I hand over my card and begrudgingly make the payment. The old guy then takes me, through a small gate to the side of the big metal ones, to where my car is. I sarcastically thank him and he heads back to his little cabin to open the gates so that I can drive out. I drive my car back to Lydia's, still seething about how much it cost. I arrive back at the flat, park the car, and literally stomp all the way up to the front door. I then have to wait for Lydia to let me in.

"Jeez, you don't look quite as happy as you did when you left," Lydia comments as she opens the door.

"I have just had to pay four hundred and fifty quid to get my car back," I tell her as I march into the flat. She stares at me with a blank expression on her face, probably wondering why the hell I have had to pay money for my car. I quickly fill her in. "Fucking Charles had it impounded at the lot. He is such a selfish prick." I am surprised that there isn't steam coming out of my ears, that's how ticked off I am.

"Oh my god. What a dick." Lydia shuts the door and I am pleased to hear that she is in agreement. Although, I don't think she would ever agree with Charles but that's beside the point.

"Yeah, well, it's done now. I can't change it." Charles has occupied more than enough of my thoughts in the last half an hour. To keep myself busy, and on schedule, I start to pick up some of the stuff that is sitting in the hall way. Time to go and do the tip run.

"Where are you going now?" Lydia asks.

"Tip run, and then I'm taking the rest to the charity shop."

"You're on a mission this morning aren't you?"

"Yeah. Best to keep busy," I say, as I exit the flat with the bags that I have picked up. It only takes a couple more trips and all of the rubbish is in my car. There is still plenty of room left so I load up the charity stuff as well. At least I can do it all in one trip now, rather than coming back here for the charity stuff. I shout to Lydia that I am leaving and she comes running from her bedroom.

"Here you go," she says as she hands me a key. "Keep this. It's your home too now, and you'll want to be able to get in if I'm not here." Lydia smiles and I take the key from her. I have my own key. I feel my mood lighten significantly.

"Thanks Lyd." My eyes start to fill at the realisation that I have somewhere that I feel I can call my 'home.' I hastily blink back tears and give Lydia a quick hug. "I know I said I would be back before you left for The Den, but I will meet you there if that's okay?"

"Okay babes. Have fun." Have fun? She must be taking the piss. There is nothing fun about a tip run. I return to the car and drive to the tip, humming along to the radio as I go. After emptying the car of the rubbish, I take the rest of the stuff to the charity shop. By the time I am done it is only half past ten. Lydia won't be at work yet, so I decide to take a quick trip to Danish to appease my caffeine needs. I park the car just outside the coffee shop. When I walk in, I see that Bonnie is working. I take my usual seat and she brings over some coffee.

"Hey girl, where have you been hiding? Haven't seen you for a few days," Bonnie says.

"Well, to cut a long story short, Charles and I broke up so I've just been busy sorting some stuff out." I don't want her to know just how eventful my life has been in the past week so I keep it simple.

"Oh, I'm sorry to hear that. This coffee is on the house." She smiles and goes to serve another customer. I sit quietly, drinking my coffee. It's nice to be out and about, and doing something normal. I look out of the window and watch all the workers and shoppers rushing around. I like people watching. I notice an elderly couple sat on one of the benches across the road from the coffee shop. They look so cute together. They are holding hands and they seem to be sat in comfortable silence. The man gives the woman a kiss on her cheek, and she smiles at him. I can see how much they love each other. It radiates from every fibre of their being. I want to have that with someone one day. Grow old and grey with them, and still be completely in love with them. Being content, happy and secure is something I yearn for. I finish my coffee and am about to stand up, when I notice Jake coming out of the estate agents just behind the elderly couple. He's with a woman. I sit back in my seat and take in every detail that I can. The woman has jet black hair that is short and spiky. She has very striking features. Her lips are full and accentuated by her deep red lipstick. Her eyes sparkle as she seems to hang on Jake's every word. He is laughing at something she is saying. My heart feels like it's being stabbed, repeatedly. I should look away, but I can't. I savour every bit of him. His silky hair, his athletic build, how good he looks in his suit, his tanned skin and his gorgeous caramel eyes. I miss those eyes. They brought me so much warmth when I was scared. I watch them both until Jake's limo pulls up and Eric gets out of the driver's seat to open the door for them. The woman slides in first and Jake follows. I wait until they have driven off before I emerge from the coffee shop. I feel like running back to Lydia's and spending the rest of the day curled up under my duvet, but I won't do that. I need to stick to my plan and go to The Den. To hell with Jake bloody Waters. If he can be happy and forget, then so can I.

Chapter Twenty-One.

I park my car at the back of The Den, in the private parking space. As I am walking around to the front of the building, I see Lydia talking to some guy by the front doors. As I get closer, I see that the guy in question is Paul, Jake's friend. *Oh god, really? It could have been any other guy in the world, but no, it has to be someone who is connected to Jake.* I can see that Lydia is flirting as she is playing with her hair and looking generally dopey eyed.

"Hey Lyd," I say as I walk up behind Paul. Paul turns around and grins at me. "Nice to see you again Paul," I say as I shake his outstretched hand. There is no point in being rude to him, he has done nothing wrong.

"Hey," he says casually.

"Hey babes. Paul has just come to see if I want to go out with him tonight." Lydia is beaming. "He's taking me to the big fancy restaurant on the other side of town." She can hardly contain her excitement, and I don't want to appear grouchy, so I join in with her enthusiasm.

"You mean Claringtons?" I ask her.

"Yeah." Lydia seems so excited, and I can't say that I blame her. Claringtons is one of the most upscale restaurants in the area.

"That's great. I hear the food is amazing." I plaster a big grin on my face. I want my friend to see that I am pleased for her. I excuse myself whilst they finish their 'moment' and I wait inside the front doors of The Den. I don't want to venture any further without Lydia by me.

She comes through the door seconds later. The dopey look is still on her face. Lydia lets me know that John, one of the security guys, is in the main room. She locks the front door behind her and motions for me to go on in. I greet John as we enter the main room. He gives us a nod and carries on with some paperwork he has set up at the bar. John is big and burly and does not look like someone that I would want to piss off. Lydia goes ahead of me and I follow her into her office. Her office is like a hive of bright colours. There is no coordination, it's just bright. The yellow walls make me want to put sunglasses on as they are verging on a neon shade. Lydia sits at her desk and I take the seat opposite her on the other side.

"Oh my god Stace, Paul is so hot. I can't believe that he just showed up like that to ask me out."

"I'm pleased for you Lyd. You deserve to be spoilt." I mean it, I really do, but I can't help feeling a little disappointed that my love life has spiralled out of control. Her smile disappears as she asks me her next question.

"Oh Stace, are you okay with all of this?"

"All of what?" I try to appear like I don't know what she is talking about.

"About Paul taking me out."

"Why wouldn't I be?" I ask innocently, although I know what she is getting at. I am going to have to pull out some amazing acting skills to convince her that I am okay with the thought of possibly seeing Jake if things work out between her and Paul.

"Come on Stace. Paul is Jake's friend, and I don't want to go out with him if it makes you feel awkward."

"Don't be silly," I reply. I am not letting my feelings for Jake stop Lydia from meeting someone who could be perfect for her. "You go and enjoy yourself. I'm looking forward to hearing all of the details when you get back." I am astounded that I can make myself sound so happy. Inside I am breaking, but I will not spoil my friend's chance of happiness. If things work out for them, I will just have to overcome my feelings for Jake. I force myself not to roll my eyes at my ridiculous thought. Put my feelings to one side? How the bloody hell am I meant to do that? I only have to look at the guy and my knees go weak.

"Great. Now that we have got that out of the way, when are you coming back to work?" I'm glad that my acting skills over the Paul issue have paid off, but my eyes widen at her suggestion of work. I thought that she was going to let me think about it. "Don't look at me like that. I will make sure that you are safe working here Stace. You were brilliant when you worked here before, and you can be again. What do you say?" I am not overly keen on the idea and Lydia seems to pick up on this from my silence. "What if I make sure that we have the same shifts together for the next few weeks to ease you back in? And, if you start to feel unsafe or threatened, then you can leave at any time."

"I don't know Lyd. I told you that I need time to think about it."

"Oh come on babes, you said that last night." She pouts at me to try and soften me up. "I also need someone to work with me on Saturday night, and I'm really hoping that it will be you. You are much more fun than the bloody agency staff I have to use."

"No pressure then," I reply, sarcastically. I need to change the subject. "I'm going to go and grab a drink. Do you want one?"

"Yes please babes," Lydia answers as she fires up her computer. "Just a diet coke though. I need to keep a clear head." I nod and leave her office to go back to the main room. I look around the place that I used to love so much. There is no sign of John in the main room, but his paperwork is still on the bar counter. I busy myself pouring mine and Lydia's drinks and I place them on the bar counter. Before I realise what I am doing, I find myself walking towards the ladies' toilets. My feet come to a stop as I stand and look down the corridor where Donnie attacked me. Flashbacks start to appear. His hands on my body. His breath on my face. His words come back to taunt me. *'You always have been a fucking tease Stacey….. She wants this just as much as I do.'* I close my eyes and try to push them away. Anger surges through me. My body starts to tremble as I fight the urge to run. I open my eyes and slowly walk down the corridor and stop at the exact spot where he had me pinned against the wall. My breathing quickens and I tell myself that he isn't here. No one is here to get me. I collect my thoughts as I realise that the anger I am feeling has replaced any fear that I had. That bastard shouldn't be allowed to taint my memories of this place. Adrenaline pulses through me as I march back to the bar, pick up mine and Lydia's drinks, and head back to her office.

"Count me in," I say, starting Lydia.

"Pardon?" she looks at me confused.

"Count me in for Saturday night. I'll be damned if I'm going to let that wanker stop me from doing a job that I enjoy." Lydia starts bouncing up and down on her seat and claps her hands together before standing up and coming over to hug me. I hold the drinks out to either side of me so as not to spill any.

"That's fab babes. It will be just like old times." I feel a new emotion flow through my body. I am ready to battle my demons. Donnie is the first one that I need to get rid of, and I think that by revisiting the scene in which he assaulted me, I am halfway there. Once I have battled that demon, I need to concentrate on battling my feelings for Jake.

Chapter Twenty-Two.

Lydia and I arrive back at the flat at six o clock. Paul is picking her up for their date at eight, so I know that the next two hours will consist of watching Lydia trying on her entire wardrobe whilst I tell her that she looks great in every outfit. She really does have some fabulous clothes. I am so glad that we are the same size, meaning that I can always borrow them to wear. Whilst Lydia has a shower, I go to my bedroom and put my pyjamas on. I intend to be a complete slob this evening. I laze around on the sofa watching re-runs of Friends as I wait for Lydia's fashion show to begin. The second episode of Friends comes on, when Lydia sweeps into the room carrying several outfits. Let the fashion show commence. It takes her an hour to choose the outfit that she is happy with. She looks gorgeous in a dark blue halter neck jumpsuit.

"You look amazing," I say to her. Her auburn hair has been styled in delicate waves, her make-up is perfect and her shoes are to die for. Silver heels that sparkle, and they are Lydia's most prized fashion possession. These shoes only ever come out for special occasions so I know that she is seriously trying to impress Paul. She finishes the outfit off with a silver clutch bag.

"Are you sure that it isn't too much?" she asks me.

"Honey, you are going to Claringtons, nothing is too much. Plus, you are going to be the most gorgeous person in the whole restaurant."

"I'm a little nervous you know." This is very unlike Lydia. She is normally very confident when it comes to men. "I really like Paul. He makes me feel different."

"That's probably because he treats you with respect Lyd. I can tell that he really likes you too. It's obvious when he looks at you." The doorbell rings, and I think Lydia is going to have a panic attack from the look on her face. "Go to the bathroom and calm down. I'll go and let him in." Lydia runs off to the bathroom and I go and answer the door. Paul stands there looking very handsome in a black shirt, black tie and charcoal grey suit. "Hey Paul, come on in. Lydia will be ready in a minute."

"Thanks." He looks on edge. Maybe he is nervous too?

"Would you like a drink whilst you wait?" I ask him.

"No, I'm good thanks." We stand awkwardly in the hall way waiting for Lydia to appear. I try to think of something to say but words evade me. I have never been one for idle chit chat. Lydia emerges from the bathroom a few moments later, and the look on Paul's face is priceless. "Wow. You look beautiful," he says as he walks up to her and places a kiss on her cheek. Lydia's cheeks blush as she thanks him.

"Okay, let's get going," she says to Paul. Paul takes Lydia's hand and leads her out of the flat. On her way out, Lydia turns and blows me a kiss.

"Have fun guys," I shout after them. I close the front door and head to the kitchen for a take away menu. I decide to order in pizza. I phone my order through to my favourite pizza place and I order my usual, a barbecue chicken pizza. I then settle back on the sofa to see what films are on. I see that Magic Mike is on so I decide to ogle Channing Tatum for the next hour or so. Twenty minutes later, there is a knock at the door. Thank god for that, my pizza has arrived and I am starving. My stomach grumbles as I grab my purse from my bedroom before I go to the front door. I am busy fumbling with my purse to pay the delivery guy as the door opens, but when I look up, I see that Jake is standing there and he is holding my pizza. I feel like the wind has been knocked out of me. I can feel my heart rate accelerating. We just stand and stare at each other. I try to calm my breathing and appear unaffected by him standing there, but I am a complete wreck at the unexpected sight of him.

"Um, Jake, why are you delivering my pizza?" I ask.

"I'm not really delivering it as such. I just........ I just........." he can't seem to find the words that he needs to say. It is now that I notice that some of Jake's confidence seems to have left him. He looks uncomfortable and is fidgeting slightly from foot to foot.

"You better come in," I say as I back away from the door to let him pass. Jake strides through the door and I close it behind him. I smell his aftershave as he walks past, and it does things to my insides. I realise at this point that I look like shit. My hair is chucked up into a ponytail and I am wearing my oversized pyjamas. *Crap, this is why you should always be prepared,* I tell myself. Although, I never thought that I would need to be prepared for Jake to show up on my doorstep so I can forgive myself for this faux pas. "Um, would you like a drink?" I ask him. I figure I need to say something in order to break the ice between us, and a drink is the only thing that comes to mind right now.

"That would be great thanks. Just a cold drink will be fine." I see his shoulders relax a little at my offer of a drink.

"Go on through to the lounge and I will bring it through." I go to the kitchen, place my purse on the side, and grab two glasses and a bottle of diet coke. My hands are shaking slightly from the shock of seeing him. What could he possibly want? I go to the lounge and set the glasses down on the coffee table. I manage to pour the drinks without spilling them everywhere, and then I take a seat on the sofa. I put my hands between my knees so that Jake can't see that I am shaking. Jake has chosen to sit in the armchair that is situated opposite the sofa. That's good. Distance is good. Jake's eyes bore into mine, but he makes no move to start a conversation. It looks like I am going to have to be the one to get the ball rolling so to speak.

"What are you doing here Jake?"

"I just wanted to see how you were doing." He looks at me with sadness in his eyes.

"Oh." A wave of disappointment goes through me. What was I hoping he would say? Was I hoping that he would grab me and make love to me as if nothing had happened? *Stop it Stacey, this is no time to be having those kind of thoughts.* I clear my throat ready to answer him. "I'm good thanks. Why wouldn't I be?"

"It's just with the way that I treated you yesterday, I thought…….."

"You thought what?" I cut him off. "That I would be a wreck? That I would be crying all over the place?" My defences rise at his presumption that I would be a mess without him in my life.

"No, I wasn't thinking that at all." Jake looks panicked. "I just don't feel that I was very fair to you. I never should have acted the way that I did. I shouldn't have treated you like that after the way things were left at my place." My mind quickly wanders back to both of us, in the bathroom, at his place. His kisses, his eyes, his body. I feel my sex clench at the mere thought of it. I need to know why he rejected me after he initiated the kiss between us. I decide to voice the issue that has been bugging me since that night.

"Why did you push me away Jake?" I need to be strong. I need to hear his explanation. Jake runs his hands through his hair and looks at the floor.

"Things are not easy for me Stacey. I have never had a connection with a woman like I have with you." I notice that I am holding my breath. I slowly exhale as I listen to his words. "I know that it sounds crazy, but it's how I feel. I pushed you away because I am scared of hurting you, and I really wanted to keep you as a friend. If things were to go further with us, then I'm afraid that you would end up hating me." Jake takes a sip of his drink before he carries on. "Although, I made you hate me anyway." He looks deep into my eyes at this point. I feel like he is looking inside my soul. My heart is pounding and adrenaline is surging through me.

"I don't hate you Jake." He looks shocked as his eyes go wide. "You have hurt me, but I don't hate you."

"Why not? I acted like a complete asshole."

"Yes you did," I agree with him. "I just think that we got carried away with our emotions that night. What with what happened with Donnie and Caitlin, I just think that we were looking for some kind of comfort. I don't think that it meant any more than that." I am lying my ass off, but I hope that I can convince him otherwise.

"Really? That's what you think?" he sounds dubious. I nod at him.

"I understand that you don't trust many people. It's obviously a difficult thing for you to put your trust in others. But, at some point Jake, you need to let go of that fear and stop pushing people away. I think our connection is strong because we are meant to be in each other's lives. We are meant to be friends. And friends mess up and then they forgive each other. That's just how it works." I smile at him and I see him physically relax in the chair.

"You mean, we can still be friends after what I did?" He looks at me like I am speaking a foreign language and he doesn't quite understand what I am saying.

"Of course we can. You kind of did me a favour actually because it made Lydia and I sort everything out."

"Glad to be of service." We both burst out laughing. I am not angry with him anymore. Now that he has explained himself, I understand why he did it. If only he had told me that to start with. I may not have known him for very long, but it's almost like there was a small void in my life without him. I may have feelings for this guy, but I would rather have him as a friend than as nothing at all.

"Want some pizza?" I ask as I open the box. The tenseness of the last ten minutes has dissipated.

"I thought you would never ask."

Chapter Twenty-Three.

I make Jake watch the whole of Magic Mike as punishment for being an ass. Needless to say, he isn't too pleased with the idea, but he's being a good sport about it. It's the least he can do. I think it's hysterical. Especially when the actors start stripping off.

"How's your arm now?" I ask him as the film comes to an end.

"It's better. I had it looked at today, and the bandage can hopefully come off in the next couple of days. The doctor seems to think that there will be minimal scarring."

"That's good news. Well, apart from the scarring part. Caitlin sure wanted to leave her mark on you, didn't she?"

"Yeah well, it's my own fault for getting involved with her in a non-professional manner."

"No it's not. Just because you don't want to be with her doesn't give her the right to go all psycho on you. You mustn't blame yourself for her poor mental health." He can't possibly think that her behaviour can be excused? I look horrified at the thought but he just hits me with his stunning smile. "Why are you smiling about it?"

"I'm not smiling about that. I'm smiling at you."

"Me?" I have no idea where he is going with this.

"Yeah, you. Even with me behaving like a bastard towards you, you're still willing to see the good in me. No one has ever been like that towards me before." My heart goes out to him. How can people not see the good in him?

"What can I say? I'm a sucker for nice eyes and a bit of charm." My tone is playful and he laughs at my statement. This feels nice, and it feels right. "So, I start work again on Saturday night."

"Where are you working?" Jake asks me.

"At The Den with Lyd."

"Seriously? Is that a good idea with what happened there?" Jake looks concerned by this turn of events.

"It's fine. I went there today with Lydia whilst she was catching up on some paperwork. I found myself standing and looking down the corridor where Donnie assaulted me. I didn't feel any fear. I just felt so angry. I used to love working there before I moved in with Charles. I don't want to let what happened with Donnie take that away from me. I've had some great memories in that place, and I don't want one bad night to taint it." I don't want Jake to try and put me off of the idea. I have made up my mind and I'm going to stick to it.

"If you're sure then I'm pleased for you. Just be careful though Stace. There are still guys out there that won't care about your personal space."

"I'll be fine. Plus, security know not to let Donnie in ever again, and I'm sure Lydia will have them keeping tabs on me to start with. I'm not going to let it break me Jake. I also need a job, and working with Lyd again will be awesome."

"Any trouble and I want you to call me. I mean it." Jake looks and sounds deadly serious. His intense gaze is a little bit arousing. I feel a strange sense of comfort knowing that he is worried about me. It's crazy how we have got past our falling out like it never happened.

"Okay." I smile at him and he grins back at me like a Cheshire cat. A worried looking Cheshire cat that is. "So what........" I am cut off by the sound of the front door opening. I hear Lydia giggling. "Sounds like they had a good time," I say to Jake. Lydia and Paul walk into the lounge with massive smiles on their faces. When Lydia clocks Jake though, her mouth drops open.

"Oh, hey guys," she says. She surveys the scene and studies us both in turn. "Am I sensing something going on here?" I need to shut down her active imagination, and quick.

"If you are sensing that Jake came by to apologise and then we ate pizza and watched a film, then you would be correct."

"Oh right. Sooooo, you two are all good now?" Lydia sounds a little wary and is looking at me for an answer.

"Yeah we're fine Lyd. Jake knows that he was a complete idiot for the way he acted."

"Hey!" Jake feigns a look of hurt. I roll my eyes at him.

"What? It's the truth," I say, smiling.

"Yeah, I have to agree with Stacey on this one Jake," Lydia chimes in.

"Okay, I think that's enough for one night," Jake says as he stands up. "I think it's time for this idiot to leave." He's being playful and I love it. I stand up as Jake walks to the lounge doorway. "Are you staying Paul?"

"Uh...........," Paul looks dumbfounded at Jake's question.

"We're just gonna have a night cap before Paul goes home," Lydia says, coming to Paul's rescue. I resist the urge to laugh and Jake smirks, giving me a wink.

"Well, enjoy your night cap guys. Do you want to see me out Stace?"

"Sure." I get up off of the sofa and follow Jake to the front door. He opens it and then turns around and gives me a hug. I stiffen to start with, but I soon relax as his body presses against mine. What I wouldn't give to be in the same situation as Lydia and Paul right now.

"Thank you for forgiving me," Jake whispers in my ear.

"You still need to make it up to me Waters. Magic Mike and a pizza just doesn't cut it," I whisper back jokingly. Jake stands back and releases me.

"Hmmmmmm. I will have to think about that one. Good night Stace."

"Night Jake." Jake turns, opens the front door and leaves. I close the front door behind him and lean against it. I collect my thoughts for a few moments before I go to tell Lydia that I am going to bed. I reach the lounge doorway and see Paul and Lydia kissing on the sofa. I decide to just go to my bedroom without disturbing them. I get into bed with a smile on my face. Today has been a productive day. I have my car back, I have a job, and I have Jake back in my life. For the first time in nearly a week, I go to sleep feeling content with my life.

Chapter Twenty-Four.

I wake up feeling as fresh as a daisy. I had a great night's sleep. Today is Saturday and I have my first shift back at The Den tonight. I am up, showered and dressed when Lydia comes walking into the kitchen.

"Good morning," I chirp at her. The smile she has on her face makes it look like she slept with a hanger in her mouth.

"Morning babes."

"I take it last night ended well then?" As if I even need her to answer that.

"Ssssshhhhh, keep your voice down. Paul's still in my bedroom."

"You minx," I tease her. "Is Paul staying for breakfast?"

"I don't know. He's still asleep."

"Well, just in case, how about I go out and pick us up some fresh pastries?"

"That sounds divine. Make mine a cream cheese bagel please." Lydia is practically drooling at the mouth. I finish my cup of coffee and go to put my shoes on. Today I have opted to wear my skinny jeans, black vest top, black blazer and black kitten heels. Wearing a blazer makes me feel confident and kind of sexy. My hair is loose and wavy. I grab my sunglasses, purse and phone and I head out of the front door. I arrive at Danish and order some croissants and bagels, as well as some full fat latte's.

Bonnie isn't working today so I take a seat and people watch whilst I am waiting for the food and drinks. It is a gorgeous morning. The sun is shining and it seems to make my mood even brighter. I am called to collect the food when it's ready and I leave the coffee shop and go back towards the flat. I hear my phone beep to notify me that I have a text message. I stop walking and balance all of the food and drinks in one hand, so that I can retrieve my phone from my back pocket. I see that I have a message from a number that I don't recognise. I unlock the phone and read what it says.

Good morning Miss Paris. You are looking well

this morning x x x

I glance around me, but I don't see anyone. *Who the hell is this from?* They obviously know who I am, and whoever it is, they have my phone number and they can clearly see me right now. Panic grips me. I furiously look around again, trying to see any signs of the person it could be when, suddenly, someone taps me from behind, on my shoulder. I shriek, drop the drinks and food on the floor and spin around. Standing there, looking a little shocked at my reaction, is Jake. All at once I feel fear, anger and stupidity.

"What the hell were you doing Jake? You scared the shit out of me!" I shriek at him. He looks dumbfounded. His mouth is opening and closing like a fish.

As I start to calm down a little and the anger fades away, I suddenly start to laugh hysterically. I laugh so much that my sides begin to ache from it. Jake just watches me, and he looks even more shocked than he did before. I bet to him, and anyone else that might be watching, I look like a lunatic. This thought, of course, makes me laugh even harder.

"Uh, Stace? Are you okay?" Jake sounds nervous, which I guess anyone would be when their friend seems to have lost the plot.

"Yeah. Yeah, I'm okay. Just, don't ever do that to me again," I say, once I have calmed down enough to form a sentence. I take off my sunglasses and wipe tears from my eyes. I then playfully smack Jake on the chest.

"Hey! There's no need for that."

"Oh I think there is Mr Waters. I presume that this message is from you?" I thrust my phone in front of his face with the offending text message on the screen so that he can read it.

"Guilty." He holds his hands up in admission. "I didn't expect you to react like that though."

"It was just the look on your face. Priceless." I look down to the spilled drinks and the food strewn over the pavement. "Well, you have just ruined breakfast for the happy couple."

"Lydia and Paul?" he asks me. I nod to clarify that I am indeed talking about Lydia and Paul. "Oh shit, I'm sorry. I'll go and buy some more to replace them."

"No, don't worry about it. They're probably far too busy in the bedroom again to be honest."

"Things went well last night for them then?"

"I would say so, yes." I feel happy for my friend. She deserves to be with someone who is going to treat her right. There is however, still a little part of me that wishes that I was being made to feel like that right now. I missed out on so much whilst I wasted my time staying with Charles.

"Well, if they are going to be busy for a while, why don't I take you for breakfast? I have a meeting to get to in about an hour, but we have time to grab something if you want to?" Jake says. I pick up the food and drinks from the floor and dump them in the nearest bin.

"Well, when you put it like that, how can a girl refuse?" I let my playfulness take over. "Come on Mr Waters, but you're buying." Jake holds his arm out for me to link my arm through. I oblige and instantly feel the warmth that radiates from his body. It makes me feel safe. "How did you get my phone number anyway? I don't recall ever giving it to you."

"I have my ways Miss Paris." Jake winks at me. Why do his words not faze me in the slightest? I don't even really care how he got my number to be honest. I'm just glad that he has it. We end up going into Danish. The waitress looks at me a little oddly as I was only in here about ten minutes ago. I order a black coffee and a pain au chocolat and Jake then places his order.

"So, what's your meeting about today?" I ask him. I want to get to know as much as I can about him, even if that does involve discussing his schedule for the day.

"It's actually not the best meeting to be going to in the world. I have to fire someone today."

"Oh no, why?" I never comprehended that Jake would be the one to have to fire staff.

"Well, this is off the record obviously, but this person has been leaking information to another company. And not just any company, but one I am trying to acquire." Jake seems a tad timid saying the last part. My brain twigs straight away.

"You mean Charles' company, don't you?"

"Um…….. yeah." He looks very uncomfortable discussing this.

"It's okay, you don't have to look so worried. I have no loyalties to that man at all. But, I feel I should tell you that, he's never going to sell his company to you. He told me, when we were together. His mother and him are not your biggest fans." I don't feel bad about telling Jake this information. He should know if he is wasting his time, which I think that he is.

"Hmmmmmm. There are ways and means of persuasion. I just haven't found out what Charles' is yet." Jake then tells me the tactics that he has used so far, and I have to say that I'm a little unimpressed that he hasn't done his homework of Charles better. My lips start to twitch as I realise that I can actually help Jake with this matter. The question is though, even after everything Charles did to me, can I really help Jake out? I don't want to seem bitter, but I reach my decision very quickly.

"I'm a little disappointed Waters," I tease.

"How so?" He looks intrigued.

"Well, a man of your intellect, I would have thought that you would have found out what makes Charles tick by now."

"Tick?"

"Yeah. What buttons you have to push in order to help get what you want."

"Oh no. I don't want you to give me advice Stace." Our waitress brings over our orders interrupting our conversation. We politely thank her whilst she drools over Jake. When she walks away our conversation continues.

"Why the hell not?" I reply, referring to his last statement.

"Because, I don't want to get you involved in this. He's your ex-boyfriend, and I don't want you to feel uncomfortable by divulging anything. I would never ask that of you." I feel touched that he wants to keep me out of it, but I want to help him with this.

"Look, we're friends, and friends help each other out. There's nothing more to it than that." Apart from maybe a little satisfaction on my part that Charles will finally get his comeuppance, but I'm not going to admit that.

"Really? Nothing more to it?"

"Nope." He doesn't look convinced at my answer at all. "Look, I'm not about to divulge any big secrets as I don't know half of what Charles gets up to. The only thing I am going to say to you is, Charles' reputation and status is more important to him than anything. Maybe you need to dig a bit deeper into what prompted me to leave Charles." I leave it at that and I see Jake wrestling with himself to leave the conversation, or to ask more questions.

"And that's it?" he asks incredulously.

"Yep." I take a bite of my food and then pick up my coffee. "One of two things will happen. You will either use this new information to help you to acquire the company, or it will tarnish Charles' reputation so much that you will acquire some of his business. Either way seems somewhat of a bonus, don't you think?" Jake leans back in his chair and I can see him processing what I have said. He starts to smirk and I return that with a cheeky grin.

"I like the way you think Miss Paris," Jake says, making me feel a little bit smug. After what Charles put me through, he deserves a little pay back.

Chapter Twenty-Five.

Jake walks me back to the flat after we are finished up in Danish. I feel a little sad that he has to go. I've enjoyed our time together.

"Want to come in and wait for your ride?" I ask him.

"No, it's okay. Eric will be here any moment now."

"Oh, okay." I try not to sound too disappointed. "Well, I best go in and explain to the happy couple what happened to their first lot of breakfast, and why it has taken so long for me to return." Jake replaced the food and drinks that he made me drop earlier on, even though I told him not to worry about it.

"Tell them that I will make it up to them sometime," Jake says. With that, his limo pulls up alongside the curb and Jake gestures for Eric to remain in the driver's seat. "So, I'll see you soon?"

"Sure. Now, go and kick ass at your meeting," I reply. I bet he looks hot as hell when he's in boss mode. He smiles at me and I turn to walk to the flat.

"Hey Stace," Jake shouts at me, making me turn back around to face him. "Good luck with your shift tonight. You're gonna do great." I just smile at him as he gets into the limo. Eric catches my eye, and I can see him smiling. I wonder what he's so happy about? He nods in my direction and I give him a little wave. I watch as the limo pulls away. I know that Jake is watching me from inside, even if I can't see through the blacked out windows that conceal him. I can just feel it. My insides do a little flutter, but they quickly disappear as I see a blonde woman stood across the road, peering out from behind a tree. A feeling of familiarity washes over me. *Oh my god, it's Caitlin! What the hell is she doing?* I feel a sense of unease creep over me. I close my eyes and re-open them a few seconds later, to discover that she has disappeared. I scan the street and all over the other side of the road, but there is no sign of her. I shake my head. I must be seeing things. I do another check before turning to enter the block of flats. I feel a little shaky at seeing the image of Caitlin. Do I phone Jake and tell him? *No Stacey, don't be stupid. You're just seeing things. There is no need to worry over this.* I reach the flat and unlock the front door. As soon as I have shut the front door, I hear Lydia's voice shout to me.

"Where the bloody hell have you been? We're starving." I walk in the direction of her voice and I see her and Paul sat at the kitchen table.

"Sorry guys," I say as I put their bag of food and tray of drinks down on the table. "You'll have to ask Jake why I was delayed." I smirk at them both and go to my bedroom without explaining any further. Without knowing the full story, they will be able to come to their own conclusions about why I was gone for so long. I know that Lydia will have so many different scenarios running through her head about what may have happened. I shouldn't leave her in suspense, but it doesn't hurt to keep some things a mystery. Jake and I may only have gone for a bit of breakfast, but to me, it was the best breakfast that I have ever had. Just being near him makes me feel special.

How he has this effect on me, I will never know. My bubble is quickly burst as the image of Caitlin, stood across the road, pops into my mind. It can't have been her. Why the hell would she be stood across the road, peeking out from behind a tree? I am definitely seeing things. I must be. I shake my head and turn on my laptop. I take off my shoes and blazer and make myself comfy on my bed. I need to spend some time working on my novel. I decide to re-read what I have done so far to distract me from my overactive imagination. I need to get back into my writing groove and get my novel finished.

Before I know it two hours have passed, and I have added another couple of chapters. Feeling pleased with myself, I take a bathroom break and get myself a glass of diet coke. I glance at the clock and see that I have three hours before I need to be at work. I can hear Lydia and Paul in the bedroom. *Jeez, how are they able to keep going? They have been holed up in there, near enough, all day.* Actually, I don't think that I want that question answering. I go back to my bedroom and rifle through my clothes to pick out an outfit to wear tonight. I settle for black skinny jeans, a white sleeveless shirt and black boots. I don't want to flash too much flesh. I still feel a bit wary about being too revealing, so a shirt is perfect. I go to take a shower as Paul emerges from Lydia's bedroom.

"Oh, uh……..Hi Stace," he says, awkwardly, as he runs one hand through his hair.

"Hi Paul. You guys finished in there yet?" His cheeks suddenly turn a rather bright shade of red.

"Um………… yeah………. I'm………. I'm just leaving actually."

"Well okay then. Enjoy the rest of your day." Paul scurries off, puts his shoes on and leaves the flat. I chuckle to myself at his flustered behaviour. I continue to the bathroom and take a shower. By the time that I have showered, dressed and finished sprucing myself up, I look confident and assured. I have tied my hair up into a ponytail and I have only applied minimal make-up. I don't want to attract any unnecessary attention so I figure that remaining low key is best. I put everything that I need in my handbag and I watch some television, in the lounge, until Lydia is ready to leave. Thoughts of Caitlin return to my mind as I am sat there waiting. *How would she have known where to look for Jake? She can only have been following him, surely? She must be really messed up to act in the way that she does. Maybe she doesn't realise that she's behaving like a loony?* I shake my head as the questions come thick and fast. *Stacey, you were just seeing things. Of course Caitlin wasn't there. It's either your mind or your eyes playing tricks. There is no need to be worried about this.* I convince myself that I was imagining things. I push any thoughts of Caitlin to the back of mind. It is now quarter past six and we need to be at work by seven. I go to see what Lydia is doing and to tell her to get a move on. I open Lydia's bedroom door and see that she is putting her make-up on.

"Are you nearly ready to go?" I ask her. Lydia finishes applying her red lipstick and pouts in the mirror.

"Ready when you are babes."

"Finally," I exclaim. I just want to get to work and get started. I feel a little anxious and I need to keep myself busy. Eventually, we get to the bar at quarter to seven. In all honesty, I did think we were going to get here later than that, seeing as Lydia was a tad behind schedule, so it's not too bad. Lydia and I go and put our handbags in her office and then I follow her to the bar area. I stand behind the counter and instantly I feel at home. The bar acts as a barrier, so it kind of makes me feel protected to a certain extent. The place isn't busy yet, but give it another hour and I know that it will be four people deep at the bar. I grab myself a bottle of water out of the fridge, and Lydia quickly updates me on anything that has changed since I left six months ago. I listen intently, determination coursing through me that I am going to do a good job tonight. An hour and a half into my shift, I have no time to think about anything other than cocktails. It seems Lydia forgot to mention to me that I would be chief cocktail maker. After making what feels like my thousandth cocktail of the night, I need a break. I pass cocktail duties to a girl named Penelope, and I go to collect some glasses from the various tables around the room. I watch some of the people as they dance together. They all look so carefree. Either that or the alcohol has well and truly taken effect on them. I pick up as many glasses as I can carry and I start to walk back to the bar. As I am walking, I feel someone pinch my bum. Rage courses through my entire body. I literally dump the empty glasses on the nearest table and I whirl around to see who the culprit is. I come face to face with some young lad, who can't be a day over the age of twenty-one. He is grinning at me and sweating profusely. *Ugh, is this really attractive to anyone?*

"Hey there gorgeous. How about we have a little bump and grind?" He slurs each and every word. I resist the urge to slap him around the face for his inappropriate touching.

"No thanks," I reply in a pissed off voice. "And can I just say that, for future reference, if you ever touch my ass again, I'll pound *your* ass into the ground." The guy looks seriously shocked, even in his inebriated state. It's almost like he is trying to decide whether he imagined what I said, or if I did actually say it. "Are you having some trouble understanding what I said?"

"N......nnn.......no," he replies, putting his hands up as he starts to back away. Who do these men think they are? It's almost like they think they have a green light to touch a woman wherever and whenever they want to. I stand straighter and turn to the table that I placed the glasses on. I pick the glasses up and smile to myself as I carry them to the bar. *See, that wasn't so bad was it Stace? You handled that really well. You threatened to beat up a teeny bopper but hey, it worked.* My conscious starts to make me feel bad for being quite so short with the guy. I shrug off the nagging voice and see that I am due my twenty-minute break. I tell the other bar staff that I am going to Lydia's office to take my break. I pour myself a diet coke and take it with me. I open Lydia's office door and the smell of Chinese food hits me. As the room comes into full view, I see Lydia has some company. Paul and Jake are sat there, eating from Chinese take-away cartons.

"Can anyone join this private party? Or is it invite only?" I ask. My mouth starts to water from the aroma of the food. Well, I presume it's the food, it could of course be the sight of Jake sat there. He looks good in his suit trousers and white shirt, which has the top two buttons undone. *My, my, my, very tasty.*

"Nah, we can allow you to gate crash," Lydia's answer interrupts my thoughts.

"Well jeez, thanks so much," I reply sarcastically. I sit on the empty chair, which is next to Jake, and I take the spring roll that he is about to eat out of his hand.

"Hey," Jake says.

"What?" I say innocently, as I take a bite of the spring roll. Jake smiles.

"Don't worry, we didn't forget about you. Your food is in this bag," he says as he lifts a bag from the desk and hands it to me. I lick my lips and take a carton out of the bag. I delve straight into the carton to see that it is chicken chow mein. "Wow, someone is hungry."

"Yeah, I am starving. I didn't eat before I came to work and I've been busting my butt out there." The others all stare at me in amazement. "What?" I say once I have swallowed my mouthful of food.

"You know, for someone with such a cute little figure, you sure can eat Stace," Lydia gawps at me as I shove noodles into my mouth. The food may not be piping hot, but it still satisfies my taste buds.

"Oh shut up. Anyway, what are you all doing in here? And Lydia, do you realise how busy it is out there? I really don't think that the other bar staff can cope."

"The staff will be fine, they do it all the time. The customers aren't going to leave as they are all too pissed to go anywhere else by now. And as for what we are doing, we are eating Chinese food. Isn't that obvious?"

"Oh ha ha, very funny," I reply, sarcasm once again taking over my tone.

"Actually, I wanted to drop by and see Lyd, so I text her and Jake happened to be with me. We thought that we would grab some food on the way," Paul says.

"Uh huh," I reply. He's a really bad liar. I decide to bite the bullet and voice why I think they are really here. Well, why Jake is here anyway. "So, no one has come here to check up on how I'm coping then?" I direct my question at Jake. He averts his eyes away from me, confirming what I suspected. "I thought so. You guys really need to think of better excuses. And I'm doing fine by the way."

"I know, I saw you tell that guy that you would put him on his ass," Jake chuckles. I stare open mouthed at him. "Remind me never to pinch your ass," he teases.

"How the hell did you know that?" I ask.

"Oh, I was coming back from the toilets when I saw the confrontation happen. I must say, I'm impressed. I don't think that he will be bothering you again." Lydia and Paul burst out laughing and I can't help but smile. Warmth courses through my body from the people sat in this room. This is how my life should be. A life full of laughter, love and friendship.

Chapter Twenty-Six.

I wake up on Sunday morning and my feet are throbbing. Wearing high heeled boots for my first shift back at The Den was not my best idea. I forgot how excruciating the pain can be. I get out of bed and make my way to the bathroom. After using the facilities and splashing some cold water on my face, I head to the kitchen to make some strong coffee. It is only nine in the morning, meaning that I have only had four hours' sleep. I make my coffee and go back to my bedroom to lie down on the bed. I smile to myself as I settle back under my quilt. My first shift back was brilliant. It has boosted my confidence significantly. It was also kind of sweet that Jake came to check up on me, but I'm not going to tell him that. My phone buzzes to notify me that I have received a text message.

Good morning sunshine. I hope that you are well rested because we are going out for the day. Be ready for 11am. I will have Eric pick you up in the limo. Jake x

What the hell? Why is he taking me out? Actually I don't care why, but it would be nice to have some sort of clue as to what he has planned. I text back.

Morning Mr Waters. And where might

we be going? Stace x

It only takes a few seconds for him to reply.

Don't ask questions. All will be revealed

soon........ Jake x

So much for trying to get information out of him. I jump back out of bed, take a few sips of coffee and then I rush into the bathroom. I shower at the speed of lightening. When I return to my room I am faced with choosing what outfit to wear. With no idea of where Jake is taking me, I choose something simple. I put on my white sundress and team it with my sandals and white cardigan. I leave my hair to dry in waves and I apply some mascara and lip gloss. The whole time my mind is conjuring up different ideas of what Jake might have planned. I wonder if he does this kind of thing with all of his friends? *Don't read too much into it Stace. He has made his feelings clear about just being friends.* I take one more look at myself in the mirror and then I go and knock on Lydia's bedroom door, so that I can tell her that I am going out. I enter before being told to and am confronted by the vision of her and Paul in a very compromising position.

"Ahhhh," I shriek. They both stare in my direction and I quickly shut the door. I squeeze my eyes shut and try to erase what I just saw. "Sorry guys," I yell so they can hear me. "I'll um, I'll leave you to it." Shit, I was not expecting to see Paul's bare butt at this time on a Sunday morning. Actually, I never thought I would see Paul's bare butt at all! How awkward! I didn't even realise that he had stayed the night. I thought that he was just seeing Lydia to the front door for a good night kiss. I was so exhausted last night that as soon as I got in, I got changed into my pyjamas and went straight to sleep. Hence why I didn't hear a thing. I sit on the sofa in the lounge and clock watch until it gets to eleven o clock. The doorbell rings at the exact time stated in Jake's message. I grab my bag and answer the door. Eric is standing there, dressed in a smart suit.

"Miss Stacey," he smiles. "Mr Waters is waiting for you. Please follow me to the limo." I shut the front door behind me and do as he asks. I resist the urge to laugh at his tone. He sounds so serious.

"Eric, there really is no need to be so formal around me." I get the feeling that my comment falls on deaf ears. Eric strikes me as very old school when it comes to manners etc. "Where am I being taken to?"

"I'm afraid I can't tell you that Miss Stacey. Top secret." He winks at me as he answers.

"Uh huh." I get into the limo and pull my phone out of my bag.

Jake, are you going to tell me what's

going on? I'm not a great fan of

surprises. Stace x

I hit the send button and wait for a reply. I get nothing back which irritates me. I'm not used to people surprising me. The usual surprises I tend to get are generally bad ones. This better be good. I sit in the limo, with my arms folded, waiting to see where I am going. Eventually, Eric pulls up in front of a clothes shop. And not just any clothes shop. It just so happens that we are in front of the most expensive clothes shop in the county. I gawp as Eric opens the limo door for me. I step out and my eyes instantly find the gorgeous outfits that are on display in the window.

"Here we are Miss Stacey. Jake is waiting inside for you." I open and close my mouth a few times before I can speak.

"Uh, thanks," I say. Eric nods his head and then returns to the limo. I watch as he drives away and then I turn back to look at the big gold plated front doors of the clothes shop. I have never set foot in here before. *What the hell has Jake brought me here for? Why a clothes shop? I thought guys hated shopping?* I approach the building and a doorman, who I hadn't noticed before, opens one of the doors for me.

"Good morning," the doorman says.

"Uh, morning." I smile sheepishly and walk through the door. As I enter, I instantly feel underdressed. The women are dressed in designer outfits, and the men are all in designer suits. Even the few children that are in here are immaculately dressed. Not a pair of trainers in sight. I look down to my clothes and gulp. My high street sun dress just doesn't cut it in here. I get a few snotty looks as I wander around the ground floor trying to find Jake. A woman approaches me as I get half way through the store, and I think that she is coming to tell me that I am in the wrong place.

"Are you Miss Paris?" she asks me.

"Yes." I look at her name tag which says her name is Gloria.

"Please follow me. Mr Waters is waiting for you on floor five." Gloria then turns and I obediently follow her. She doesn't give off a very friendly vibe and it makes me feel uncomfortable. I survey the clothes as we walk to the lifts and each item I see is more exquisite than the last. I bet the price tags are pretty too. When we get to the lifts, Gloria presses the button and we wait. When the lift arrives, I get in but Gloria remains where she is.

"Remember, floor number five is where you will find Mr Waters," Gloria says. I press the number five button and when I look up, Gloria has disappeared. Thankfully I am in the lift on my own, so there are no eyes judging my choice of attire. I take a few deep breaths as I try to calm myself. My heart is beating a little faster than usual and I think it's a mixture of excitement at what Jake might have planned, and also a touch of nerves as I feel so out of place. The lift doors ping open when I reach floor five. I step out and see some of the most gorgeous dresses that I have ever set my sights on. However, none of them are as gorgeous as the man approaching me. Jake is wearing a navy blue suit and white shirt with open collar. He looks incredible. He smiles at me and I almost melt. As he reaches me he gives me a hug.

"Hi. Are you okay?" he asks.

"Not really Jake. I am dressed completely wrong. You could have given me a clue as to what to wear. The looks that I got off of some of the people shopping, when I entered, were looks of complete disgust. What the hell am I doing here?"

"You look beautiful. There is nothing wrong with what you are wearing." Jake gives my body a quick perusal and I feel my sex begin to stir. His gaze makes my body feel alive. I need to keep myself in check. We're friends and nothing more. "Oh, and I brought you here to ask you a favour," Jake says. He appears to have finished looking at my outfit and seems ready to get to the point of this outing. I raise my eyebrows in question. "I have an event to attend this evening, and I was hoping that you would accompany me. If you say yes, then I want you to pick out one of these dresses as a thank you for coming with me." My mouth drops open. He wants to buy me one of these dresses? Wow, I wasn't expecting that.

"And what if I say no?" I decide to tease him for a moment. It's the least he deserves after not warning me about what to wear here.

"Well, then I guess I will just have to try and change your mind." I swear I see a mischievous glint in his eye, but I choose to ignore it. I can't let myself think that anything is going to happen between us.

"Hmmmm, now that could be interesting," I reply. I appear thoughtful for a few moments before giving him my decision. "Of course I will go with you, but you don't need to buy me one of these dresses. They are so expensive. I can't let you spend that kind of money on me."

"Why not? You would be doing me a favour and for that, I would like to get you something. In this case, the something, is a dress."

"But……"

"No buts. If you don't want to choose a dress then that's fine, I'll just have one picked out for you." Jake smirks as I scowl at the sneaky sod. Either way it looks like I am getting a new dress from here. Seeing as he hasn't given me much choice, I might as well take a look around myself.

"What's the event for?" I ask.

"It's just some corporate thing that I need to attend."

"Oooohhh, sounds so exciting," I mirror his unexcited tone and Jake laughs.

"This is why you will be perfect as my plus one. You are just as excited by the thought as I am." Now it's my turn to laugh.

"You drive a hard bargain Mr Waters," I tease.

"I'm sure the dresses did most of the persuading for me," he smirks. "Now go and have a look around and see what catches your eye. Don't take any notice of the price tag either." He gives me a stern look. I almost feel like I am being told off. "I will be waiting at the chairs outside the changing rooms." Jake then turns and leaves me standing like a lost lamb in the aisle. I slowly start to walk around and study the dresses on display. How am I meant to know which dresses to try on? They are all so gorgeous. As I continue to look lost, an older lady approaches me.

"Can I be of help dear?" she asks. She has white hair which has been tied back into a neat bun, and she has a kind face. Very different from Gloria's overall vibe.

"Oh, I'm just looking around. I'm not exactly sure where to start though, everything is so beautiful."

"Would you like me to help you? My name's Edele and I am one of the personal assistants here." She smiles at me and holds her hand out for me to shake.

"That would be great, thank you." I feel very grateful that I am going to have some help. Thirty minutes' pass by and Edele has helped me choose ten dresses to try on. Edele actually picked out most of them. She clearly knows what she is doing as I like each and every one of them. I pass Jake as I walk into the changing rooms and I give him a smile. He is busy talking on his mobile phone, but he still smiles at me. I enter a changing cubicle, which is massive. It even has a plush armchair in the corner. Mirrors adorn each wall of the cubicle and the lighting is subtle. It is a vast difference from the harsh, bright lights of the high street changing rooms.

"If you need any help getting into any of the dresses, then there is a bell you can press just by the mirror there," Edele says as she points to the button. "I will only be outside the changing rooms anyway." I thank her and she draws a deep, purple velvet curtain across the cubicle so that I have some privacy. I eye each dress and pick the first one that I want to try on. It is a floor length, halter neck, red dress. It is lovely, but it isn't really fitting my figure the way in which I would like it to. I take the dress off and try on a further three before deciding that those aren't right either. I want a dress that is going to blow Jake's mind. Just because we are friends, it doesn't mean that I can't make myself look as good as possible around him. The fifth dress I decide to try on is one of the dresses that I picked out myself. It is gorgeous. It is a floor length, strapless navy blue, silk gown with a thigh high slit. It is simple and made of the softest material. I slip it on, do up the side zip and gasp as I look at myself in the mirror. The dress hugs my body in all the right places, and it compliments my blue eyes. I press the button to call Edele in to see what her opinion is. I draw back the curtain and wait for her. She appears seconds later and gasps when she sees me.

"Oh my, that dress is perfect. It fits you like a glove, and it looks like it was made for you," she says.

"Thanks Edele. I like this one too." I am so pleased to hear that Edele is in agreement with me about how good the dress looks. Of course, she may be working on commission, but I don't let that thought cloud my judgement of her. I twirl around and survey myself in the mirrors once more. "I don't think that I need to try on any of the other dresses. This is the one that I want."

"Well then my dear, this one it shall be. It is stunning. I will have it boxed up for you once you have changed out of it," Edele says.

"Okay." I pull the curtain back across the changing room and I carefully take the dress off. I put my white sundress back on and open the curtain to hand Edele the navy blue dress. "Um, could you not let Mr Waters see it please? He's the guy sat in the chair out the front. I would like to keep the dress as a surprise until I wear it."

"Of course. If I must say, he isn't going to know what's hit him when he sees you in this." Edele takes the dress and I smile at her compliment. Edele then exits the changing rooms. I slip my sandals back on and leave the other dresses where they are. I exit the changing rooms to see that Jake is now tapping away on his iPad. He looks up at me as I approach him.

"Have you chosen a dress?" he asks, looking to my hands and finding them empty.

"I sure have," I say grinning.

"Well, that didn't take as long as I thought it was going to. Where is it?"

"Edele is packing it for me."

"Do I not get to see it?"

"Nope. You will just have to wait until tonight." I feel a little bit of excitement at the suspense of making him wait.

"That's not fair." He pouts playfully.

"You surprised me with a shopping trip, and now I get to surprise you with what dress I have chosen." I can't wait for him to see it. I hope it does the trick and accomplishes blowing Jake's mind.

"You're a tease Miss Paris."

I wink at him. "That's what makes our friendship so special."

Chapter Twenty-Seven.

Eric picks up Jake and I from the clothes shop, and drives us back to the flat. I thank Jake for the shopping trip and say good bye. I don't invite him in as I need to prepare myself for tonight. I practically jump from the limo when Eric opens the door. He hands me the box, with my dress in, and I near enough run to the block of flats and up the stairs. I can't wait to show Lydia my dress for tonight. I excitedly unlock the front door. I chuck my bag down and go through to the lounge. Lydia is dozing on the sofa, but I have to wake her.

"Lyd, wake up. I have to show you this amazing dress that I just got." She opens her eyes and groggily sits up.

"Calm down Stace. I'm exhausted," Lydia moans whilst yawning.

"Hardly surprising." I raise my eyebrows as I speak. Lydia smiles as I thrust the box, with my dress in, in her face. Her eyes go wide at the name of the clothes shop sprawled across the front.

"Holy shit."

"I know."

"Well come on then, what are you waiting for? Let me see, let me see." I knew her enthusiasm would reach its peak once she had realised where I had been. I place the box on the coffee table and undo it. I carefully take the dress out and I hold it up so that Lydia can see. Her mouth drops open.

"Oh wow! That is beautiful. Did you buy this?" she asks me. Lydia knows her fashion, so she probably has a good idea of how much this dress is likely to have cost.

"Nope. Jake bought it for me. It's to wear to some corporate event tonight. He asked me to go with him, and he said that the dress was a thank you for doing him a favour by accompanying him." I can't stop smiling. Lydia gets up off of the sofa and feels the fabric.

"Oh my, that is so soft. It's a gorgeous dress babes. So are you and Jake still maintaining that you are just friends?" she looks at me sceptically.

"Yes." Lydia cocks one of her eyebrows at me. "Honestly Lyd, he asked me *because* we are friends."

"Uh huh." I know that she isn't convinced. Hell, I don't even know if I am convinced. "Well, I wish I had friends that bought me dresses like this." I roll my eyes at her. I don't want to let myself hope that Jake and I can become more.

"Anyway, is it possible that you could help me with my hair later? I was thinking of having a classy up-do."

"Absolutely. What time are you leaving here?" Lydia's eyes sparkle with excitement.

"Jake will be picking me up at seven o clock."

"That only gives us a couple of hours. We better get started now."

"Can I grab a cup of coffee first?"

"No! You haven't got any time to waste. Now, go and get your butt in the shower so that we can get started," Lydia demands. I salute at her whilst she claps her hands together. She loves to help with things like this. I don't argue with her as I need to make sure that I look my absolute best for tonight. I go and hang the dress up in my bedroom before going to the bathroom. Whilst I am in the shower, I make sure that I am hair free in all the right places, just in case. Who's to say that I won't meet someone at the event tonight? I am kidding myself. My eyes will only be for Jake, but it doesn't hurt to be prepared. I wrap a towel around my body and exit the bathroom. On entering the lounge, I find that Lydia has set up a make shift beauty salon. One of the kitchen chairs has been placed in the middle of the room, the coffee table is covered with hair necessities, and a vast range of make-up occupies the remaining space. Lydia hands me a glass of wine and gestures for me to sit on the chair. I smile at her and take a sip of my wine. Lydia goes out of the room as I take my seat and wait to see what she is doing. Lydia returns a few moments later with even more hair products.

"Christ Lyd, I don't want to look like a poodle," I tease her.

"Shut up and let the magic happen." She takes a sip of her wine and then, somehow, finds an empty spot on the coffee table to place her glass on. I close my eyes as Lydia works her magic. After what feels like hours of drying, curling and adding god knows what products to my hair, she has finally finished. "That's it. I'm done. Go and take a look." I get up and head for the mirror hanging in the hall way. I don't know what I am expecting to see, but my hair looks awesome. Lydia has put it into a classy up-do like I wanted, and she has left a few loose curls hanging down so that they frame my face in just the right places. I run back to the lounge and give Lydia a bear hug. "Easy, you don't want to spoil your hair," she says in between laughing at me. "Now, what are you thinking of doing make-up wise?"

"I thought that I would just do some eye shadow, mascara and lip gloss."

"Oh jeez, it's a good job that you have me here." Lydia sighs and manoeuvres me back onto the chair. She starts selecting various make-up items from the table and then stands in front of me. "Now, close your eyes and don't open them until I say so."

"Yes ma'am," I say with a smirk. I feel various brushes touch my face but I have no idea what I am going to look like. I'm not one for wearing much make-up at the best of times so I don't know how I am going to look. By the time Lydia says that I can open my eyes, it is quarter to seven. I hope that I look okay as I don't have the time to re-do anything. I get up from the chair and go back to the hall way mirror. As I stare at my reflection, I can't quite believe what I'm seeing. Lydia has used the subtlest grey eyeshadow, and my eyelashes look longer and thicker than normal. She has highlighted my cheekbones and coated my lips in a nude coloured lip-gloss. I stare, open mouthed at her handiwork. I look to the lounge door and see that Lydia is leaning against the door frame.

"You like?" she asks me.

"I love it. Thank you." I go to hug her again but she stops me by holding her hands up in front of her.

"You only have ten minutes to get yourself into that dress and get your shoes on. We can save the hugging and general worshipping of me until later." I smile at her, as I quickly go and put the dress on, which is in my bedroom. I find my grey stilettos out of their hiding place, and I put those on too. I decide not to take a clutch bag with me. I don't need to take a phone or anything so I don't need to bother carrying a bag. I forgo wearing a jacket because I don't want to cover the dress up. I walk out of my bedroom and Lydia gasps.

"Wow Stace, you are going to knock all those people dead tonight." I look at myself in the mirror. I look like a different person. I feel like some sort of princess in my dress. I do a slow twirl, surveying myself from all angles, when there is a knock at the door which makes me jump.

"Shit! He's here, he's here," I say, starting to panic.

"Calm down babes. You're all ready to go. I can't wait to see the look on his face when you open the door." I scowl at her as I know that she is convinced that there is something going on with Jake and I.

"Knock it off Lyd. We're just friends."

"Yeah, yeah. You keep telling yourself that." I ignore her comment and go to answer the door. As I open it, I can smell Jake's aftershave. God he smells divine. Jake is looking at the floor when I open the door. He slowly lifts his head and I feel his eyes rake over my body. As he meets my gaze, I almost orgasm. Butterflies start to dance in my belly and my breathing becomes shallow. Jake appears to be lost for words so he just smiles at me. A genuine, heartfelt smile. He looks absolutely gorgeous in his black tuxedo.

"Hi Jake," I manage to say. Jake clears his throat before he answers.

"Stacey," he nods his head as he says my name. "Are you ready to go?" I can't mistake the heat lurking in his gaze.

"I sure am," I reply, sounding much more confident than I feel. I turn around to Lyd who is standing there with a goofy grin plastered on her face. "Don't forget to leave the door on the catch," I say to her.

"Okay. Have fun guys. Don't do anything that I wouldn't do," I hear her shout as the front door closes behind me. We walk out to the limo and Jake places his hand at the small of my back. He leans in and whispers in my ear.

"You look incredible." I feel his breath on my cheek and it makes me shiver in delight.

"You don't look so bad yourself." I look at him and we mirror each other's smiles. As we reach the limo, Eric opens the door for us to get in.

"Miss Stacey," he says in greeting. "You look beautiful this evening."

"Thanks Eric." I enter the limo and Jake follows me. He takes the seat beside me. We set off and there is complete silence between us. I can feel the sexual tension mounting and I start to feel slightly awkward as Jake just gazes out of the window. I fiddle with my hands the whole time. The limo pulls to a stop, only a short while later, and I feel a sense of unease. *Maybe Jake doesn't like my dress? Maybe he thinks that it's too much? Maybe I shouldn't have come to this event with him?* As I ponder these questions in my head, Eric opens the door for us to exit the limo. I take a deep breath and follow Jake out of the limo. I look around and can't see anywhere that looks like there is an event going on.

"I will give you a call when we are ready to leave," I hear Jake say to Eric in the background. I then feel his hand take mine and he leads me to the building situated in front of us. It's just an office block. This is a strange place to hold an event. As we enter the lobby it becomes clear to me that this is Jake's offices. The giant letters behind the reception desk are a big giveaway seeing as they say WATERS INDUSTRIES. *Oh great, I have got all dressed up just to come to Jake's offices.* Jake leads me to the lift at the far end of the reception area. He presses the button to call the lift and we wait for the doors to open. We are the only ones waiting and it seems to take an age for the lift doors to open. We enter the lift and Jake presses the button for the top floor. The doors close and I decide that I have had enough of the tension between us.

"Jake, is something wrong?" I ask. He turns and faces me.

"No, nothing is wrong. Should there be?"

"It's just that, you have hardly said two words to me since you picked me up. Have I done something to upset you? Did I pick the wrong dress?"

"God no. You picked the perfect dress, trust me. And you certainly haven't done anything to upset me. I'm sorry, I'm just thinking about tonight. I hate having to schmooze with people that have no personal regard to my life. To be honest, I can't stand most of the people coming, but business is business."

"Oh, right. Okay then." I can't think of anything else to say to that. I turn to face the lift doors and I wait for us to reach the relevant floor. We finally reach floor number thirty-two and the lift doors open. Jake still has hold of my hand and he leads us into the huge open plan room. There is classical music playing and there appears to be about a hundred people chatting amongst little groups. The whole space has been decorated to reflect an intimate vibe, but to be honest, I think it looks a little tacky. I instantly think of Martin and of how much better he would have made this place look. I must give him a call and arrange to meet him for a catch up.

"Show time," Jake says, breaking my thoughts. I can tell that he doesn't want to be here by the tone of his voice. As a few people start to notice Jake, they begin to come over to him. I am casually pushed aside by the people, mostly women, who want to get his attention. Jake didn't mention that all of these people were going to be assholes with no manners. I leave him to it and walk over to the bar area that has been set up. I order a glass of white wine and take a grateful sip when it is delivered to me. I am quite happily sipping my wine when I see a familiar face emerge from the throngs of people. *Oh fucking great. This is all I need.*

"Well, well, well. Look who it is," says Charles sarcastically.

"Hello Charles." I am completely caught off guard. Jake never mentioned that Charles would be here. I don't even pretend to make my greeting sound genuine. Charles is wearing a dull grey suit with tweed patches at the elbows. He looks awful. How I ever slept with this guy is baffling.

"So, what brings you here?" he says as his eyes peruse my body. I involuntarily shiver from his gaze, but not in a good way. The guy still knows how to make me cringe.

"I came with Jake." I can see Charles' face change instantly from smug to shocked.

"You……… you came with who?" he stutters.

"Jake. Jake Waters." It actually feels good to shock him.

"So it was you who gave him information on me then?"

"What?"

"You told him about why we split up didn't you?" Charles' face starts to go a little red.

"I most certainly did not." I actually didn't tell him the reason, I just hinted that he should look into it, but I'm not about to tell Charles that.

"You lying bitch. It must have been you." Charles looks infuriated and I'm starting to get the impression that he is going to be volatile towards me.

"Charles, I never told Jake why we split up. If Jake found out, then he found out another way." Charles is going to believe what he likes but I feel like I must stand my ground.

"Rubbish. You have betrayed me. Why on earth would you come here with him, knowing that I was going to be here?"

"I didn't know that you were going to be here actually. Believe it or not Charles, I don't plan my life around your every move anymore." This guy really does think that he is a god. "And for your information, I came with Jake because we are *friends*."

"Pfft," Charles scoffs. "Well, did you know that your *friend* has taken half of my clients? Your *friend* is trying to put me out of business, all because I won't let him buy my company. You really think he made friends with you on the off chance, and that he has no ulterior motive? He is simply using you to get to me."

"Is that so?" God, he really is an egotistical pig.

"Yeah. He couldn't give a shit about you, and you have fallen for his charm hook line and sinker. You really are fucking stupid aren't you?" Charles snarls at me. I feel anger start to rise within me. *Who the hell does he think he is talking to me like this?* I need to keep my cool, but it is proving difficult right now.

"You can think, and say, what you like Charles. I have no interest in pandering to your paranoia. Jake and I don't even talk about you. You are irrelevant to my life, and you have been for quite some time." There is so much more that I could say to Charles at this point, but I don't want to be the one to cause an unnecessary scene. I don't need to have an argument with him. Charles is part of my past, and I intend for him to stay that way.

"You are a nasty piece of work Stacey Paris. What the hell did I ever see in you? I gave you everything and you just threw it back in my face. You are just a user and............" Charles doesn't get to finish his sentence because Jake has grabbed his arm and spun him around.

"I suggest you leave, *now,*" Jake says as he looks at Charles like he is a parasite. Other guests are starting to look over, but I don't think Jake cares about that.

"I'm not going anywhere. I was invited here by your company, remember? I am just telling Stacey some home truths. It's not my problem if she doesn't like to hear them."

"Okay, let me make this clear to you Charles. You were never supposed to be invited, but I guess your name was left on one of the mailing lists. That's the only reason you got an invite. And don't worry, I will be having a word with the person who sent the invites out. Maybe they will come to you for a job when I'm finished with them?

Secondly, you do not get to speak to Stacey like that. She is here as a special guest of mine and if you disrespect her, then you disrespect me. Thirdly, I suggest that you put your drink down and get the hell out of here, before I throw you out myself." Jake's stance is intimidating and Charles physically shrinks back in shock. Charles turns to the bar, and with shaky hands, puts his glass down. He doesn't look at me as he does. He then turns back to Jake and excuses himself. Charles then heads for the lift and Jake watches him, until the lift doors shut, erasing Charles from our sight. I think that Charles made a very wise decision to get out of here when Jake told him to. I have seen Jake in action when someone pisses him off, and it's not pleasant for the receiver. Jake's gaze locks with mine and I mouth a thank you to him. He comes closer to me so that he can whisper in my ear.

"Give me half an hour and then we're out of here."

"Okay," I reply. I watch him as he strides across the room and starts chatting to a couple of older guys. I feel so aroused by his protectiveness of me. I suddenly find myself swamped by people wanting to talk to me about Jake's little display with Charles. I try to avoid answering their questions and opt for polite chit chat instead. However, I'm not really listening to what any of them are saying. I am too busy studying Jake. I feel a flutter as our eyes connect across the room. His eyes are filled with heat, and I'm sure that mine reflect that feeling also. He looks up and down my body and then points to the lift. I look at him a little confused and he again just points to the lift. I make my excuses to the cling on that is trying to ask questions about Jake, and I do as I am told. I press the button to call the lift and I wait for the doors to open. I enter the lift when it's ready and Jake comes bounding in just as the doors are beginning to close. He stops in front of me and then without warning, pushes me against the wall of the lift. My heart is racing. I can feel the heat from his body. My sex is crying out for him. He leans closer to my face, but I stop him from getting any closer by placing my hand on his chest. I need to make sure that he isn't going to run away this time.

"Are you sure about this Jake? I don't want a repeat of last time." Even though my body craves this man's touch, I am wary. Understandable seeing as he freaked out after our last kiss. My heart is pounding as I wait for him to answer me. I am willing him, with every fibre of my being, to say that he is sure about this. About us. He looks intently at me and studies my face before he answers.

"I was a fool last time. I can't fight it anymore. I want you Stacey. I need you." His words undo me. It's all I need to hear. I put my hands behind his neck and bring his face closer to mine. As we are about to kiss, the lift stops and the doors begin to open. We jump apart and a group of four people get in and stand in front of us. Damn them. Just as things were about to get physical, we get interrupted. The sexual tension in this lift is unbearable. I need to get out of here. I need to feel Jake's hands on me again. The lift seems to take forever to reach the ground floor. When it finally does, Jake puts his arm around my waist and guides us to the exit of the building. His limo is already outside, waiting at the curb for us. Eric greets us and hold the door open for us to get in. I can barely contain my excitement at the thought of what might happen. Jake sits opposite me this time and simply says four words that are like music to my ears. "Your place or mine?"

"Yours."

Chapter Twenty-Eight.

We get back to Jake's house and barely make it through the front door before his lips find mine. Our kiss starts out soft but quickly becomes frenzied. It's like we can't get enough of each other. All the pent-up frustration of the last few weeks have come to a head. Jake puts his hands on my ass and lifts me up so that I am straddling his torso. Thank god I picked a dress with a thigh high split. Although, if I had chosen a dress that was going to rip, I don't think I would even care at this moment in time. He carries me up the two flights of stairs, our lips never leaving one another, and he takes me into his bedroom. He lies me down on the bed and then breaks our kiss. I let out a little moan at the loss of contact. Jake stares down at me and begins to speak.

"You are so beautiful," he whispers to me. He strokes my cheek as I lean my face into his hand. He stands up and takes his suit jacket off. I quickly sit up and stop his hands as he reaches the top button of his shirt.

"Let me," I say, in my most seductive voice. He lets his hands fall to his sides as I begin to undo his buttons, slowly. When I am done, I stand up and slide the shirt down his arms. The material falls to the floor and I place my hands on his chest. His muscles ripple and it take all of my willpower not to hurry things along. I want to savour every moment of this. My hands make their way down to his trousers and I unbuckle them. They fall to the floor and Jake steps out of them before kicking them to one side. My hands find the rim of his boxers, but he steps back, halting my progress.

"You have too many layers on. Let's even things out and remove this dress." He takes hold of hands and moves my arms so that I am holding them above my head. He then finds the side zip and slowly undoes it. He then pushes the material of the dress down my body, until it is pooling at my feet. I stand there, with just a pair of white lace knickers on, and my shoes. Jake nods approvingly. "You are breath taking." I feel my legs quiver at his sensual words. I can't speak. A part of me is, subconsciously, waiting for him to run again. I hope that he doesn't. I don't think that I could bare it if he walked away a second time. His hands skim up the sides of my body until he reaches my breasts. He gently caresses them as he leans down to kiss my neck. I close my eyes and put all thoughts of him running away to the back of my mind. I feel his lips trail across my skin until they reach my right nipple. He gently licks and sucks, which heightens how turned on I am right now. I can't think straight. Jake proceeds to do the same to the other nipple before he finds my lips again. We kiss and his hands travel back down my body until his fingers hook into the sides of my knickers. Before I know what is happening, Jake has ripped the lace from my body and thrown the knickers onto the floor. He then pushes me back onto the bed and lifts one of my legs into the air so that he can take my shoe off. He repeats the same manoeuvre with the other leg before swiftly removing his boxers and climbing on top of me.

"I'm going to make you scream my name Stacey." I gasp at his words and stroke his back with my nails, enjoying the feel of goose-bumps on his skin. Jake continues his delicious torture by kissing a trail all the way down my body, finally reaching my most intimate place. He pushes my legs apart so that I am spread before him. He gently parts my folds and softly blows on my clit before licking it with his tongue. As he starts to swirl his tongue around in circles, I feel my insides start to tighten, bringing me closer to orgasm. He pushes his fingers inside me and I am done for. I scream out his name as he continues to pleasure me until I have ridden out my orgasm. He makes his way back up my body and smirks. I feel his erection pushing against my opening. No words are needed as he slowly enters me. The feel of him inside me is like pure bliss. My fingers grip his strong arms as he starts off with a slow rhythm. He returns his mouth to my nipples and gently bites them. I grip his arms harder as I urge him to go faster. His speed picks up pace and I start to pant as I can feel another orgasm approaching. *Another one? Well, this is new.* Never in my life have I come more than once during a sexual encounter before.

"Look at me," Jake says. My eyelids are heavy, but I manage to open them fully so that I can look at him. His eyes capture me. His caramel pools sparking various emotions within me. Jake continues to increase his speed and I know that I can't hold on much longer.

"Jake, I'm nearly there," I say breathlessly. This seems to spur him on even more. His lips crash onto mine and I moan into his mouth. Whilst he continues to pound into me, he moves one of his hands and places his thumb on my clit. He then moves his thumb in small circles and I break our kiss to shout out his name again. I can feel that he is getting close as his breathing has changed. I tighten all of my muscles, gripping around him to heighten our combined pleasure.

"Come now Stacey," Jake says on a growl. I obey and let myself be taken into oblivion by him. He finds his release at the same time. We both cry out until our orgasms are complete. Jake collapses on top of me as we both try to regain our breath. "I have been waiting for that for so long," Jake says, his face buried into my neck. I lie there feeling more than satisfied. I remember how he made me feel all those months ago, when he was just some one-night stand, but those feelings are nothing compared to what I am experiencing right now. This man is perfect. Emotion threatens to overtake me as I try to divert my thoughts from how strongly I feel for him. This moment is one that I will never forget. I will certainly accompany him to more events in the future if this is how they all end.

Chapter Twenty-Nine.

I wake up to find that I am alone in Jake's bed. I immediately sit up, covering myself with the duvet. I strain my ears in order to hear any noises. I don't hear anything. *Shit, what have I done? Jake is obviously regretting what happened last night, otherwise he would be here. Oh no Stacey, you bloody idiot. You were friends with him but you couldn't just leave it at that, could you?* I am silently cursing myself at how stupid I have been to give into my feelings for him. I hang my head and wonder how on earth I am going to prepare myself for the rejection all over again. *Why did you have to cross the line and sleep with him?* Now I will have definitely lost him as a friend, as well as anything else. As I am about to climb out of the bed, Jake walks into the bedroom whistling to himself. Oh my. He is standing there, holding a tray with what appears to be breakfast food on it, in just his boxers. My eyes drink in his magnificent form. He smiles and walks over to the bed.

"I have made some breakfast in the form of coffee and toast. I hope that this is to madam's satisfaction?" He's in a playful mood. Thank god for that.

"Well, one can't have smoked salmon every day," I tease back. We both laugh and relief rushes through me. *He's still here. He hasn't run off.* Jake places the tray at the end of the bed. He then climbs in next to me, leans over and kisses me passionately. I return the kiss and feel my sex start to awaken. He slowly pulls back, breaking our connection too quickly for my liking.

"Good morning Miss Paris."

"Good morning yourself."

"I think that breakfast can wait a while," he says, making me feel excited. He moves the breakfast tray from the bed and onto the floor. He then pulls the duvet off of me and pulls me on top of him. He settles back on the bed so that his back is leaning against the head board. I grin and move my lips so that they connect with his skin. I start by kissing down from his neck, and I keep going until I am level with his boxers. I gesture for Jake to lift his bum so that I can remove his boxers. He obliges and I quickly get the material out of my way. Without any warning, I take him fully into my mouth.

"Holy shit," he says as he grips the headboard above him with both hands. I move up and down his length and swirl my tongue across the tip. Jake's moaning turns me on even more. I've never enjoyed this activity before, but now, I can't get enough. I grab his balls with my hand and gently massage, feeling his legs stiffen as I do. "Fuck Stace," is all I hear before I feel him release his load into my mouth. I drink every drop and then kiss my way back up his body. "Well," he says, a little out of breath. "That is something that I could wake up to every morning."

"Play your cards right Jake and it might just happen." I appear to have turned into a kinky bitch in the space of a few hours. Jake flips me on my back so that he is on top of me, and enters me hard without any warning. I let out a yelp at the sudden intrusion, but it is an intrusion that is most welcome. He pumps into me, bringing me to orgasm quickly. He follows a few strokes later. Jake climbs off of me and turns me so that I am lying on my side, facing away from him. He then settles behind me and pulls me into his arms. I love the feel of him wrapped around me so I nuzzle into him as much as I possibly can.

"Mmmmmm," he says as he nibbles gently on my ear lobe. "Now that is a great start to the day." I giggle, but it is brought to an abrupt halt by the realisation that we haven't used a condom. *Oh my god, how could I have been so careless? And how did I not realise this before now?*

"Jake, we haven't used a condom," I say, panic evident in my voice.

"Are you on the pill?" Jake inquires.

"Well, yes but………."

"Then there's nothing to worry about. I had a check done just before I last slept with you, and I haven't been with anyone since. I'm all clean," Jake states confidently. *Phew, well, there's a relief.* "How about you?"

"I was checked after Charles and I split up. All clean."

"Well then, there really is nothing to worry about." I relax against his chest. It isn't exactly the most romantic conversation that I have ever had, but I feel better knowing that he has been checked out. I feel so safe, here in his arms, and in his bed. This must be what heaven feels like. I am definitely floating on cloud nine this morning. "Would you like some coffee now?" Jake asks me.

"Yes please," I answer. Jake sits up, picks up the breakfast tray and places it on the bed. I make myself comfy by leaning against the head board, mirroring Jake's position. He hands me a cup of coffee and I gratefully take a sip. The coffee is just as delicious as I remember it, even if it is only luke-warm. Jake picks up a piece of cold toast and takes a bite. He screws his face up and puts the toast back on the plate.

"Yuck," he says as I laugh at him. He looks so cute with his face all screwed up. "I'm going to go and pick us up some proper breakfast. Would madam like to order anything in particular?"

"Surprise me."

"I thought you didn't like surprises?" he lifts one eyebrow in question.

"I don't as a rule. But, your surprises have all been good so far so I figure I can change my mind." Jake gives me a quick kiss and gets out of bed. He puts on a pair of jeans and a t-shirt. He fails to put any boxers on.

"I won't be long. Don't move." He points his finger at me and I salute. I hear him leave the house a few moments later. I do move as I need to use the bathroom. When I have finished, I return to the bed. I am so happy. Jake has made me feel like this. I replay the events of last night when Jake's phone ringing breaks my thoughts. He obviously forgot to take it with him. I reach for his phone, which is on the bedside table, and see that Caitlin is calling him. I put the phone back down in disgust. *Why is she still ringing him? Hasn't she got the message yet?* I decide to try and not let her get to me. I don't want anything or anyone to spoil this moment of happiness. I lie down and doze until I hear Jake return. He runs into the bedroom a few moments later, and launches himself onto the bed. I scream as I think that he is going to smash into me. He manages to miss, but he quickly crawls over me and pins me to the bed.

"Did you move?" he asks, playfully.

"Only to use the bathroom," I reply.

"Hmmmmm. I'll let you off on that one. Breakfast time." Jake gets back off of the bed and goes to the bedroom door. I now see that he dropped a brown paper bag before launching himself onto the bed. He comes back over and starts pulling food trays out of the bag. My stomach starts to grumble in anticipation of the great smelling food. I pick up one of the food trays and see that it is full of scrambled egg. I start to eat some, when Jake's phone starts to ring again. Jake picks it up, sighs and cuts the call off.

"You okay?" I ask him. I don't want to look like I am prying into his life. I want him to tell me because he wants to.

"Yeah. It's just Caitlin. She keeps bothering me." Good start, he has been honest with me. "She just doesn't want to leave me alone. I'm consulting a solicitor about her next week." I stop eating the eggs and turn to look at him.

"Seriously?"

"Yeah. This shit has been going on for too long. Caitlin needs help, but she won't listen. The only thing I can do now is take legal action." Well, I wasn't expecting that answer, but I am pleased that he is going to be taking action to stop her from contacting him. I finish my eggs and eat a couple of strips of crispy bacon before admitting defeat over being able to eat anything else. Jake's phone rings another three times before he decides to switch it off. I can sense how irritated he is so I suggest taking a shower to try to distract him. My idea works as he carries me to the ensuite and we re-explore each other's bodies in the giant walk in shower.

Chapter Thirty.

"Fuck," is all I hear Jake say from the bedroom, before I hear him run into the hall way and down the stairs. I am getting dried after a steamy shower so I have no idea what Jake is swearing at. I stand there, stunned by his outburst. I don't have to put my dress back on from last night as I have found a pair of leggings that are mine from when I was staying here before. Luckily for me they were missed during the packing up of my belongings. I borrow one of Jake's shirts, which is huge on me, and I button it up to just above my breasts. I run a hairbrush through my hair and go down the stairs to see what is wrong. I get to the kitchen and can hear voices coming from outside. I walk to the huge Patio doors, which look onto the garden, and see Caitlin. *Really? Does this girl have nothing better to do with her time?* I stop myself from walking outside, just in case Jake doesn't want me to interrupt their conversation. I hide behind the curtain and just listen.

"Jake, why are you doing this to me? I need you. Can't you see that I need you? Is it that slut that you had here the other week? Is she the reason that we're not together? I'll take her out if you need me to?" *Oh fuck me, this girl really is a lunatic.* I stand frozen on the spot.

"You need to watch your mouth right now," Jake says, and he sounds mad. "Get the fuck off of my property Caitlin. I don't want you here."

"Jake, we can work this out. Come on, we're good together." Caitlin is pleading and it sounds desperate. I feel a little sad for her that her life has come to this.

"I'm going to see a solicitor next week to get you out of my life. You need help Caitlin. You're not well."

"No," I hear Caitlin start to sob. "Please Jake, don't do this. I love you."

"Well I don't love you. How many more times do I need to tell you that? You just refuse to listen to me. I have tried being nice about this, but you are leaving me no choice but to go down the legal route." I can hear him getting exasperated, so I decide to go and see if I can help. This may be one of my stupidest ideas yet, but I feel I need to do something. My legs start to move and I approach Jake and Caitlin with slight caution. Jake's eyes go wide when he sees me. Caitlin has her back to me so she hasn't noticed me yet. I get up behind her and tap her on her shoulder. She whirls around and her eyes narrow at the sight of me. Before she can say anything, and before I can lose my nerve, I start to speak.

"I have already called the police, so if you don't want to be arrested, then I suggest that you leave. Right now." I wait for her to hurl abuse at me. The seconds tick by slowly, but she doesn't say anything to me. Instead, she turns around and walks away. I watch her as she gets to the back gate and slams it shut behind her. Well, that was far easier than I thought it would be. I was expecting her to have a full scale fit about me being here. I look to Jake who I staring open mouthed at me. "You're welcome," I say as I head back inside, appearing far more confident than I feel.

"Are you insane?" Jake asks me as he follows behind me.

"No. I just thought that you needed a little bit of help to get rid of her."

"Oh Stacey," Jake says, running his hands through his hair. "What have you done?"

"I've got rid of her, that's what I've done. You clearly weren't having any luck in doing so." I feel my defences start to kick in.

"She is messed up, and I don't want her anywhere near you." Jake walks to me and puts his arms around my waist. I put my hands on his shoulders and I place a light kiss on his lips.

"Stop worrying. She's gone. End of story."

"I don't want you caught up in this." He sounds genuinely worried.

"The sooner you see your solicitor, the better it will be."

"Yeah, I know. I'm going to call him and move the appointment up to tomorrow. I also need to get some security installed here."

"What, like cameras?"

"Yes babe, cameras. And whatever else I think I might need." Jake smiles at me and I melt against his body. "Fancy going out for some dinner?" he changes the topic and I am grateful to not have to discuss Caitlin anymore.

"Sure, but I can't wear your shirt out."

"I think you look sexy in my shirt. Makes me feel like you're mine," Jake growls.

"Yours? I'm not your property Mr Waters."

"I know that, but it feels like you belong to me. Like we were meant to be together." Jake kisses me roughly and I lose myself in his embrace. I can feel his hard length through his jeans. *How the hell can he be ready to go again?* I pull back and look at him questioningly.

"Seriously? Again?" I ask. Jake gives me a cocky grin.

"You know, we haven't christened the kitchen yet," Jake says in his seductive tone. Oh my! Jake picks me up and places me on the kitchen island so that I am sitting on the edge. "Now, you were saying something about not being able to wear this shirt. How about we remedy that and get rid of it?" Jake doesn't wait for my answer. He doesn't even undo the buttons. He just rips the shirt open, causing me to gasp in shock. He pulls the shirt off of my arms and caresses my breasts. I lean into his touch and close my eyes. His touch feels so good. His lips cover mine, and his tongue delves into my mouth. I can't help but let out a small moan. Jake lifts me up slightly, and I make quick work of pulling my leggings below my ass. Jake pulls back from me and removes my leggings completely. He looks a bit shocked as he realises that I'm not wearing any knickers. He gives me a lop-sided smile and I feel my cheeks blush.

"Very sexy," he says as he manoeuvres me so that I am lying flat on the kitchen island. The cold surface makes me draw in a breath and goose-bumps cover my body. Jake then moves his head between my legs and lets his tongue sweep over my highly sensitive clit. He moves his tongue in circles and my hands reach down to caress the back of his head. I can't get enough of him. i whimper as I feel myself approaching climax. I moan his name softly and he applies more pressure with his tongue taking me closer to my undoing. Just as I am building to my climax, Jake pulls away and quickly undoes his jeans, freeing his erection. He pushes into me and places one thumb on my clit. I am quickly transported to another world as his punishing rhythm makes me start to tremble. The shudders rack my body as I build back up to my release. I can hear Jake's breathing change to signal that he is close to finding his peak. I cry out as I feel myself free falling through my orgasm. Jake reaches his seconds later and I feel his juices pump into me. Jake slowly brings us down from our climaxes and I lie there, once again, in a state of complete bliss. Jake pulls out of me and pulls his jeans up, but leaves them undone. I lazily sit up on the counter and retrieve his shirt to put on. Even though the buttons are broken, I can wrap it around me.

"At this rate, we're never going to make it to dinner," I say. Jake pulls me off of the island and I wrap my legs around him. He carries me up the bedroom and heads for his ensuite.

"Another shower?" he asks me.

"If you insist."

Chapter Thirty-One.

I finally make it back to Lydia's at six o clock. I am exhausted as I climb the stairs, but my time spent with Jake was worth every second. I open the front door, which is on the latch, and Jake follows behind me. Lydia comes marching into the hall way.

"Where the bloody hell have you been?" she glares at me. "I have been trying to get hold of you all bloody day."

"Sorry Lyd. I left my phone here, remember?" I feel like I am about to be told off by a parent with the look she is giving me.

"You could have called me from another phone you know?" she folds her arms across her chest and starts to tap her foot.

"I've, uh, been a little preoccupied."

"Too preoccupied to use a phone?"

"Uh..........." I'm not quite sure what to say to her. I'm not used to Lydia reprimanding me for not phoning her. Lydia looks from me to Jake and her lips start to twitch.

"Oh, I see. You two finally came to your senses and got it on then?" she smirks and I feel my cheeks flush. I hear Jake chuckle as I mentally scold my best friend for being so out spoken.

"Uh, you could say that. Anyway, I've just come to get changed and then we're heading out to dinner," I tell her. I turn and grab Jake's hand and I pull him into my bedroom. I shut the door behind me so that we can have a bit of privacy from Lydia's intense gaze. "I'm sorry about that. Lydia can be a bit........."

"Forward." Jake finishes my sentence for me.

"Yeah, you could say that." I grab some clean clothes and tell Jake that I am nipping to the bathroom to freshen up. I tell Jake to help himself to a drink if he wants one and I go to the bathroom. I have a quick wash and I put on my skinny jeans and a hot pink sleeveless shirt. I quickly run a brush through my hair and brush my teeth. I apply minimal make-up and then go back to my bedroom. Jake isn't in here so I presume he decided to get a drink. I take a quick look at my phone to see if I have any messages. I have missed calls from Lydia, and a message from Charles. I inwardly groan as I open the message to read it.

Stacey, I can't believe that you are friends with that man. He will hurt you. I know that he will. You have no idea who you have got yourself involved with. All I ask is that you keep your mouth shut about my personal business. Charles.

I scoff at his message. He has got a bloody nerve. Charles obviously still thinks that he has the right to tell me what to do. I put my phone, purse and keys in my little black handbag, put my back sandals on, and I go to find Jake. He is sat at the kitchen table with Lydia. Oh god, I dread to think what kind of questions she has been asking him.

"Hey, are you ready to go to dinner?" I ask him.

"Sure. You look lovely," Jake replies.

"Thanks." I then tell Lydia that I will be back at the flat after dinner. I grab my flat key on the way out and we walk to Jake's car. "So, where are we going to eat?" I ask as I climb into the passenger seat of Jake's BMW X5.

"I thought that we could go to a little American diner that I know of. It's nothing fancy, but the food is delicious."

"Sounds good to me." I'm not one for posh restaurants anyway. I like to feel comfortable, not judged by other diners. I am so hungry though that I don't think I would care if it was just a portion of chips from the local chippy. After all of the sex today, I completely forgot about eating anything after breakfast. Although Jake mentioned going to get food earlier, we got a bit carried away, and food was the last thing on either of our minds. We arrive at the diner and wait to be seated. The waitress soon comes over and leads us to a booth at the rear of the diner. The smells all around me make my stomach grumble. I peruse the menu and decide to order a bowl of chilli with cheese fries. I figure that with all the working out Jake and I have done today, I can afford to eat the calories. The waitress comes back to our table and takes our order. Jake orders a foot-long hot dog and fries. I only order a diet coke to drink, as I want to keep a clear head. I want to remember everything about this day and drinking alcohol may distort my view of it. Jake and I chat, about nothing in particular, until the waitress has returned with our drinks. When she has left, the conversation turns more serious.

"So," Jake says. "What are your plans for next weekend?"

"No idea. I need to go to The Den tomorrow and see what shifts Lydia has put me down for. I can't really plan anything until I have done that. Why?" I ask, curiously.

"I thought that we could go away for the weekend. Somewhere where we won't be interrupted." Jake raises his eyebrows and I instantly know what he is getting at.

"Oh," is all I can say. *He wants to take me away?* This reaction to us hooking up is so different to what happened the other week. I am thrown by his suggestion and I don't really know what to say to him. Jake starts to look a little worried when I don't say anything else. Our food arrives, letting me ponder his suggestion for a little bit longer. "Listen Jake, what happened between us last night, and today, has been wonderful, but don't you think that it might be rushing things by going away together? I mean, it was only a short while ago that you told me that you only wanted to be friends." I hope he understands why I have some reservations about the idea.

"I get that, but I wasn't in the right head space then."

"It wasn't that long ago Jake, and you seem to have done a complete one eighty on me. It's a pretty quick turnaround." I say, as I pop a cheese fry in my mouth.

"I know what it must look like to you, but I was scared before. My feelings were so strong that I didn't know how to act around you." Jake grabs my hand across the table and penetrates me with his gaze. "I know that I hurt you before, and I can't apologise enough for that. I just......... I've never felt this way before. I was trying to fight it because we haven't known each other that long, but I can't. I don't want to fight it. This is all new to me Stace, but I love the way that you make me feel. I love the way that we are when we are together. I just want to prove to you that I mean every word that I say." *Wow! I am speechless. He feels as strongly as I do by the sounds of it.* "I don't want to come across as being too pushy, but why wait? Why should we take things slow? At the risk of sounding even more soppy, I feel like we were meant to find each other Stace." *Fuck me.* I am blown away by his honesty. I feel tears prick the backs of my eyes. I always thought that 'love at first sight' was a load of rubbish, but the way I feel about Jake has shown me that the saying can be true. I clear my throat and give Jake a smile.

"Let me see what shifts I am working and then we can see if we can plan something," I reply. Jake smiles and it makes my heart melt a little.

"Great. Now, eat up, you're going to need to keep your strength up." I feel my sex clench and a shiver runs up and down my spine. I have a feeling that I will be having trouble walking tomorrow if we keep this up. The rest of the meal goes smoothly, and the conversation is so easy and comfortable. I could literally talk to Jake about anything. I don't feel that he is going to judge me in the slightest. We wrap up our meal and I decline the offer of a pudding. I am way too full after eating most of my chilli and cheese fries. Jake refuses to let me pay anything for the meal. I try to argue with him, but his stern glare soon makes me give up trying. When he has paid, we leave the diner and Jake takes my hand as we walk back to his car. I have never felt so content with a man before. As we approach Jake's car, a flash of blonde hair catches my eye across the road. I stop walking and scan the other side of the road. There is nothing. No one in sight. *That's weird. I could have sworn that someone was there.* I feel a chill go through me as my mind, once again, tries to convince me that it was Caitlin. I feel Jake tugging on my hand and I look up at him. I force a smile on my face as I don't want Jake to think that I am going mad.

"What's wrong?" he asks me.

"Nothing."

"Really? Then why do you look like you have just seen a ghost?" I rack my brains for an excuse as to why I'm being so paranoid.

"It's nothing, honestly. I just feel really tired all of a sudden."

"Tired huh?" Jake doesn't believe me, but I don't want to give him cause to worry.

"It's hardly surprising really is it?"

"Hmmmmm." Jake takes me into his arms and places a light kiss on my lips. "Well, if that's all it is, then we better get you back home." I kiss him again and then we resume walking to his car. Jake opens the passenger door for me and I slide in, grateful for the safety of the car. I look back to where I thought I saw Caitlin, but again, there is no one there. *I need to get a grip.* Jake climbs into the driver's seat and we are soon on the way to the flat. I remain quiet on the drive back, my mind in overdrive. When we pull up to the flat, Jake exits the car and comes around to let me out of the passenger side.

"Why thank you kind sir," I tease, hoping to make up for my skittish behaviour just moments ago.

"No problem." Jake pulls me into his embrace.

"I've had a great time Jake." I reach up and lightly kiss him on the lips.

"Me too. And, don't forget to let me know what shifts you are working next weekend."

"I won't." I don't want to leave him, but I have to go and get some much needed rest. I also have to answer the many questions that Lydia will be asking me when I step through the front door. "Good night Jake."

"Night babe." Jake gives me a slow, lingering kiss, making me want to do all sorts of things to him. I push the thoughts to the back of my mind assuring myself that there will be another time to fulfil what I have in mind. I moan as Jake brings the kiss to an end. I smile at him and then break away from his embrace and head towards the flat. I practically run up the stairs and reach the flat in record time. I unlock the front door and walk in.

"Lyd, are you here?" I call out.

"In the lounge babes," she answers. I close the front door and walk to the lounge. I am pleased to see that Lydia is on her own, meaning that I won't have to answer any questions in front of anyone else. "So, are you going to fill me in now?" I'm not even sat down and she's already waiting for the details.

"Are you sure that you want to hear this now?" I tease. "I mean, it's getting late and you do have work tomorrow."

"Oh no you don't. I have been waiting for you to get back so that you can tell me what the hell is going on. Now, spill Paris." I laugh at her. Sometimes it's fun to wind her up a little. I settle myself into the chair and I tell Lydia most of what has happened so far. She gasps in various places, and I know that she is loving this. I don't go into too much detail about the sex. I want to keep some things to myself. I also leave out the part about Caitlin. I don't want Lydia to think that I am being a paranoid mess.

"It sounds like by Charles being an asshole, it gave Jake the push that he needed," Lydia ponders.

"Hmmm, maybe. I don't really care what pushed him though, I have had the best sex ever so I'm not complaining." I can't stop the smile from creeping across my face as I think back to each and every sexual encounter between Jake and I over the last twenty-four hours.

"Oh you dirty bitch," Lydia jokes. "On a more serious note though, I'm happy for you Stace. It's about time that you had some fun."

"I think so too. Anyway, I am absolutely exhausted. I need to go and get some sleep." I stand up and go to give Lydia a hug good night. I use the bathroom and then go to my bedroom. I get into my comfy pyjamas and get myself into bed. I lie awake for a while and just replay things from the last few days in my head. I never thought that I would ever be this happy. There is only one niggle in the back of my mind, and that is Caitlin. I am positive that she was there tonight. I can't shake off the feeling that she is doing this to mess with my head. She could, potentially, make things very difficult for Jake and I. I just hope that we are strong enough not to let her come between us.

Chapter Thirty-Two.

My alarm goes off at 8am. I get up, showered and dressed, and see that Lydia has already made a pot of coffee which is sitting on the kitchen table. There is no sign of Lydia though. I pour myself a drink as she comes waltzing into the kitchen.

"Morning babes," she chirps at me.

"Morning Lyd. You're cheerful this morning. Care to share?" Lydia, normally, hates early mornings so I know that something has cheered her up.

"Paul's taking me to lunch today," she beams at me.

"Things are going good with you two, aren't they?"

"They really are. I can't believe how well though. I keep waiting for something to go wrong, but in the meant time, I figure I should just enjoy myself."

"Oh Lydia, don't be so cynical. I think Paul really likes you, and you guys are good together." I wish that she wouldn't be so down on her self-worth. I'm also shocked as she has never been so nervous around another guy.

"I could say the same for you and Jake," Lydia replies. I just grin at her. I finish my cup of coffee and then we both head off to go to The Den. When we get there, we enter through the back door. Lydia locks it behind us as there will be no one else in here until later on tonight. Lydia just needs to print off the rota and put it on the notice board for the staff to see. I only accompanied her so that I could see my shifts. I need to let Jake know as soon as possible.

"Bugger," I say to myself as I see that I am working Friday and Saturday night next week.

"What's wrong?" Lydia asks in the background.

"Oh, I just uh, broke a finger nail," I lie. I don't want to sound ungrateful and start moaning to her about what I am working. She was good enough to re-employ me, so the least I can do is work the shifts that she has given me. Lydia doesn't seem to catch on to my big fat lie. I take my phone out of my pocket and send a text to Jake.

Morning handsome, I'm afraid that I am

working Friday and Saturday night next week.

Maybe we can take a reign check on going

away? Stace x

Within seconds my phone buzzes to notify me that Jake has replied.

Hmmmmm, is there no way that you can

switch your shifts? Jake x

I sigh and text back my response.

I would rather not, seeing as I have only

just started working here again. I'm sorry.

We can go another time. Stace x

I don't get a reply which makes me inwardly panic that I have pissed Jake off. I say my goodbyes to Lydia and leave her at The Den to get on with some paperwork before she meets Paul. I decide to go to Danish and treat myself to one of their caramel latte's. I arrive there, but I can't sit in my usual seat as it is already occupied. The woman occupying the table has her back to me. Whoever she is, she has long blonde hair which makes my hackles rise. As she turns around, she confirms what I already know. It's Caitlin. *Shit, what is she doing here? I've never seen her in here before.* I now know that I haven't been imagining seeing her in different places. Caitlin has been following Jake and I. I quickly change my order to a take away latte. I don't want to sit in here and drink it now. As soon as my latte is ready, I pay the money and then get the hell out of there. I feel a bit pissed off that, due to Caitlin being there, I feel that I have to leave. I turn in the direction of the flat and start walking. I get only a few paces ahead when I hear my name.

"Stacey Paris." I turn around and see that Caitlin is marching towards me. I roll my eyes and think of how to get out of this situation, and fast. *Bollocks, I really don't need this kind of hassle.* "So, I finally got you on your own. You tend to hide behind other people," she says as she stops in front of me. I straighten my stance and kick into defence mode.

"I haven't been hiding behind anyone," I reply in a firm tone. *What is this woman on about? She is nuts.* She starts to laugh and I begin to feel uneasy.

"You should be hiding." She narrows her eyes at me as she speaks. I don't want to show any fear at her words, but I'm sure the whole street can hear the pounding of my heart.

"What do you want Caitlin?" I am proud of how even I manage to make my voice sound. The last thing that I want to do is let her see that, physically, she is scaring me.

"I want you to leave Jake alone." This time it appears that it's my turn to laugh at her ridiculous request.

"He doesn't want you Caitlin. What part of that don't you understand?"

"That's only because you're hanging around. Do yourself a favour and tell him that you are no longer interested in him, before things get really nasty." With that she grins wickedly, turns on her heel and marches off in the opposite direction. I watch until she goes out of sight. I feel so shaken and I need to get somewhere safe. I manage to turn and power walk back to the flat. I keep checking behind me to make sure that she isn't following me. I reach the flat block and run up the stairs to the front door. I unlock the door and slam it behind me, making sure it is locked. I walk on shaky legs to the lounge and sit down on the sofa. I put the latte that I am still carrying, but have no desire to drink anymore, on the coffee table. I try to calm my racing heart and regulate my breathing. I tell myself over and over again that she is just trying to scare me into leaving Jake alone. Well, she succeeded in the scaring me part, not so much in the leaving Jake alone though. I pull my phone out of my bag and send Jake a message. I think he ought to know what just happened.

Hi Jake. I don't mean to bother you but,

I just had a bit of a run in with Caitlin. She

told me to stay away from you. She seriously

needs help. Call me when your free. Stacey x

I put my phone down on the coffee table and just stare at the blank television screen. It takes me a little while to completely calm down, but once I do, I switch the television on and settle myself back on the sofa. I have no plans for tonight, which isn't a bad thing. I think I would be a bit jumpy if I had to go out anywhere. I flick through the television channels and try to find something decent to watch. A knock at the door interrupts me. I feel cautious as I go to answer it, but then I reprimand myself for being so silly. I shouldn't feel afraid to open my own front door. I think that I would feel better about things if I had spoken to Jake, but he still hasn't responded to my message. Whoever is on the other side of the door knocks again. I take a deep breath and unlock the door and open it to see who it is. I am greeted by the sight of Jake in all his handsome beauty. A feeling of relief rushes through me and before I know what is happening, Jake has taken me in his arms and is hugging me tightly.

"I just got your message. I'm sorry I didn't see it sooner. I've been stuck in meetings since earlier this morning. Are you ok?" Jake says as he continues to keep me close to his body.

"Yeah, I'm fine. You don't need to worry about me." I try to appear calm about the situation. I breath in his scent as I nuzzle close.

"Of course I'm worried. Where the hell did she see you anyway?"

"I went to The Den with Lydia, which you already know about, and after that I went to Danish to get a drink. She was sitting at my usual table when I got there. I suspected it was her, but it wasn't until she turned around that I knew for sure. Anyway, when I saw it was her, I left." I pull back from Jake so that I can close the front door. I don't need any of the neighbours hearing about my life. I lock the door again, even though Jake is here. It just makes me feel a little better to have it locked. "When I left, she came after me to confront me about you. Basically, she told me to leave you alone. If I didn't, then things would get really nasty." Jake's face goes a little pale.

"Christ Stace. That's it, you're coming to stay with me. I want to make sure that she can't get to you again." I laugh at him, thinking that he may be over reacting slightly. Jake doesn't join in with my laughter. He looks deadly serious.

"Jake, I'm not going anywhere. I live here and I'm not going to let some jealous ex of yours force me out of my home. She's just making idle threats because she wants you back." I don't know who I am trying to convince more, Jake or myself.

"Well, if you're not going to come to mine, then I'm staying here the night," Jake says.

"Are you now?" I raise my eyebrows at him teasingly.

"That's not going to be a problem is it Miss Paris?" Jake asks as he closes the gap between us. Before I can answer, he pushes me against the door and kisses me. My knees weaken and I give myself to him. I have missed his lips all day so I intend to savour the feel of them. Jake pulls me away from the door whilst keeping his lips connected to mine, and carries me to my bedroom. Shutting the door behind us, he then throws me onto the bed. I squeal as he pounces over me. "I just want to keep you safe." My heart melts and I place a finger to his lips so that he stays quiet.

"I don't want to talk about that now. I just want you. All of you, inside me." I don't want to think about anything else other than what we are about to do to one another. Jake growls with appreciation. We both take our clothes off as quickly as possible and Jake slowly enters me. We only manage to make love once before I fall asleep in his warm, and safe, embrace.

Chapter Thirty-Three.

I wake up to the feel of Jake's lips on my neck. I smile and turn so that I am facing him.

"Hey babe," he says in the sexiest voice.

"Hey yourself." I give him a gentle kiss on the lips. "What time is it?"

"It's six o clock in the morning."

"What?" I have been asleep since we had sex yesterday. "I've been asleep for ages."

"You obviously needed the rest."

"Did you stay here the whole time?" I ask him.

"Yeah. I didn't want to disturb you by moving." He is so sweet. I sit up and stretch my arms.

"I can't believe that I was out for so long." I yawn and get out of the bed. I need to pee so I tell Jake that I am going to use the bathroom. I walk into the hall way after using the bathroom, and I can hear whispers coming from Lydia's bedroom which means that she has company with her. I'm guessing that her lunch date yesterday, with Paul, went well. I smile and go back to my bedroom. Jake is putting his clothes on. "What are you doing?" I ask him.

"I'm getting dressed, obviously," Jake says, smirking at me.

"Very funny. What I mean is, why are you getting dressed so early?" I already feel like I miss him and he hasn't gone yet. The feelings I am having are crazy. I have never had to deal with such strong emotions before.

"I have to go back to mine and pick up some notes for a meeting that I have this morning. I wish that I didn't have to go, but I'm meeting with my solicitor."

"About Caitlin?" I ask, hopeful that he is going to see what route he can go down to keep her away.

"Yes."

"Well then, you need to get going. The sooner the situation with her is dealt with, the better it will be for both of us."

"I know. I don't want you to worry whilst I'm gone. I would take you with me but, you don't need to hear the details of what I need to say." Jake looks a bit worried by telling me this. *Ugh, if he's talking about how he used her for sex then no, I would rather remain oblivious than hear all the details.*

"That's fine. I'm just going to chill here until I go to work later. I won't be leaving the flat until then." I'm hoping this information will put his mind at rest about the possibility of another run in with Caitlin.

"I will send Eric to pick you up and take you. No arguments." I sense from his tone that even if I try to argue I wouldn't win, so I just walk over to him and hug him.

"Okay." To be honest, it feels nice that he is looking out for me. I haven't felt this cared for in a long time. Jake kisses the tip of my nose.

"If I finish up with work on time then I will come over to The Den later."

"I will look forward to it." I take Jake's hand and lead him to the front door.

"Any signs of trouble and you are to contact me straight away."

"Mmmmm. I like this macho side of you Mr Waters," I purr at him.

"You keep talking in that sexy voice and I won't make my meeting." I grin and bat Jake away, opening the front door for him.

"Go." I order him as I point out of the front door. Jake just looks at me and smirks. "Jake Waters, will you get your butt out of here so you can make your meeting."

"I quite like this dominant side of you." I roll my eyes and chuckle as I kiss Jake good bye.

"Good luck."

"Bye babe." My heart does a little flutter and I close the door as Jake disappears down the stairs. I lock the door and go back to my bedroom. I put on some clean clothes and turn my laptop on. It's about time that I did some more writing. Whilst I am waiting for the laptop to load, I go and make a pot of coffee and take it to my room with me. I settle on my bed and put my headphones in so that I am not disturbed by any noises that Lydia and her guest may want to make.

I break for some lunch at one o clock. Lydia is yet to emerge from her bedroom as far as I am aware. When I took my headphones out, I heard someone leave the flat, but I don't know if Lydia left with them. She usually tells me if she is going out, so I presume that she is still in bed. Before going to make myself a sandwich, I go to Lydia's bedroom. I knock on her bedroom door but she doesn't call me in.

"Lyd?" I say loudly so that, if she in there, she can hear me. There is no answer but I can hear someone in there. Concerned, I open the door slightly and peak round. Lydia comes into view and she is on her own. She's on the bed, sobbing. I push the door open and walk over to her. "Lyd, whatever is the matter?" I say as I take a seat by her on the bed. My cheerful mood is suddenly plighted by the sight of my best friend crying.

"Oh Stace. I've been so bloody stupid," she blubbers at me. Lydia doesn't cry very often so I know that something bad has happened.

"Well, why don't you tell me what's bothering you? It may make you feel better to talk about whatever it is?" I try to sooth her.

"Promise you won't judge me?" she says.

"Hey, I'm your best friend. Of course I won't judge you."

"Okay." Lydia takes a deep breath and then slowly breaths it out. "Paul and I got into a fight last night. We were at The Den and he didn't like the fact that some guy was trying to chat me up. I was working so I could hardly tell the guy to go and fuck himself could I? Plus, it's part of the job sometimes. I didn't feel that he was over stepping any boundaries, so I wasn't really bothered by it. Anyway, this led to us arguing and Paul stormed out. I was so mad at him that when my shift ended, I started drinking with the guy that was trying to chat me up." A new wave of tears pours from her eyes, stopping her from continuing to speak. I let her regain some composure and then I gently prompt her to continue. "I can't even remember the guy's name Stace. I was so drunk. All I remember is that he walked me home, and then one thing led to another, and......." Lydia can't seem to finish her sentence. It dawns on me that Lydia slept with this guy, whoever he is.

"You had sex with him didn't you?" I ask her. I already know the answer, but a part of me needs her to confirm it. Lydia just nods her head at me and then hangs it in shame. "Oh Lyd." I pull her into a hug as I try to comfort her without words. Nothing I say would be able to ease the guilt that she is obviously feeling right now.

"I'm so stupid. I was just so mad at Paul, and this guy was giving me attention. I don't know what to do Stace. Do I tell Paul?" She pleads with me to give her the answers that she desperately needs, but I can't.

"That's up to you Lyd. I can't decide that for you. You need to do whatever feels right for you." It's the only advice that I can give her. I feel my heart break for my best friend. I hope that, if she decides to tell Paul, that he can forgive her. "I'm going to go and get us some nibbles and then we can just laze around all afternoon watching movies. How does that sound?"

"Sounds good." Lydia sniffles into her pillow. I leave her to go and look in the kitchen to see what we have in the cupboards. I am disappointed to see that we don't have anything decent at all. Great, now I am going to have to go out when I promised Jake that I wouldn't. The shop is only five minutes away, if I run then I can be back here in no time. It is pointless taking my car as there is no parking by the shop. With my best friend needing me to be there for her, I put on my trainers, grab my purse and keys, and leave the flat. I run all the way there and am gasping for breath by the time I enter the shop. My heart is racing as adrenaline spikes through me. I pick up a basket and quickly go down the relevant aisles for the things that I need to buy. Crisps, chocolate, popcorn and diet coke. I decide against a bottle of wine. I don't really think getting drunk is the best idea under the circumstances. I also pick up a couple of pizza's for later on. I promptly head to the till and pay for my items. I scurry out of the shop with my bags and run as fast as I can back to the flat. I have my keys ready as I reach the front door. *See, nothing to worry about Stacey. No sign that Caitlin is following you.* I enter the flat and lock the front door behind me. I take the bags of food to the kitchen and unpack them. I put the pizza's in the fridge and take everything else into the lounge with me. I call to Lydia to get her butt into the lounge. She walks in a few seconds later and is still crying. I point to the sofa where she flops down and curls into a ball. I go and grab her duvet and bring it into the lounge for us to snuggle under. I decide to put on an action movie rather than a romantic chick flick. With the current state of Lydia, I don't think she needs to see happy couples on the screen, even if it isn't real life. I pull out the DVD of Fast & Furious. I get the television set up and grab the remote controls. I settle next to Lydia and we spend the next couple of hours watching Vin Diesel on the big screen.

Chapter Thirty-Four.

Eric picks me up at half past six to take me to work. Lydia is asleep on the sofa when I leave. I am worried about her, but I feel that I should look after things at The Den so that she has one less thing to worry about at the moment. She should have been at work with me tonight, but I told her that Susie and I would manage. It's a Tuesday night and they are not generally too busy. I arrive at The Den and exit the limo.

"Thanks for the ride Eric," I say as he stands by the limo, holding the door for me.

"No problem Miss Stacey. I will be waiting out here for you when you finish your shift."

"There really is no need. It will be late and I'm sure you need to be getting home." I don't want to put Eric out any more than I have already.

"I insist," he says firmly. I think it is a bit unfair of Jake to ask him to pick me up, but I know that he won't disobey Jake's orders.

"Fine. I finish at eleven thirty."

"I will be waiting outside Miss Paris." Eric goes around the car and back to the driver's side. He is about to get in when I stop him.

"Hey, Eric?" I say.

"Yes?"

"When you speak to Mr Waters, tell him to give you a pay rise," I tease. Eric laughs and waves to me as I turn to walk into The Den. As I walk into the main room, I can see that there are only a couple of tables occupied. I wave to Susie, who is behind the bar already, and I go to Lydia's office to put my handbag safe. As I enter her office, my mobile phone starts to ring. I take it out of my pocket and see that it is Jake calling me. A smile instantly emerges on my face.

"Well hello handsome," I purr down the phone.

"What the hell do you think you are playing at?" Jake says in a pissed off tone.

"I beg your pardon?" My tone changing from playful to defensive.

"You told me that you wouldn't leave the flat today, so I will repeat my question. What the hell do you think you are playing at?" He sounds so mad.

"Jake, calm down. I only went out for a few minutes. Lydia was really upset, so I went to pick up a few bits and bobs to try and cheer her up. The shop wasn't far and I ran there and back. Nothing happened, I am fine. It's all okay." I try to sooth him with my words.

"I don't give a fuck if you think that it is okay. Don't you understand that Caitlin is a psycho? You need to keep yourself safe Stacey. Why didn't you just order some food in?" My words have had no effect on him whatsoever. Bugger.

"I don't particularly like your tone of voice Jake. My best friend needed me, and I was helping her. God knows she has helped me enough times. If you want to be childish about this, then you carry on. I don't have time to listen to you have a tantrum. I have to go. I need to start work." With that, I hang up the phone. *Who the fuck does he think he is talking to me like that? How dare he!* I am so pissed off with him. I put my phone in my handbag and leave it on Lydia's desk. I exit her office and go behind the bar to start serving some customers. I need to take my mind off of the conversation I have just had with Jake. The first hour goes slowly, but as soon as eighty thirty hits, the place is packed. I had completely forgotten that there was some sort of student celebration going on tonight. It is just Susie and I and we are overwhelmed with all of the customers. I quickly try to call some of the other staff, but there is no response from any of them. *What the bloody hell am I meant to do?* I can't call in any agency staff as I don't have the relevant details to hand, and I certainly can't go to Lydia's office and leave Susie on her own whilst I look for them. Susie and I try to work as quick as we can so that we can keep all the customers happy. Everything seems to be going okay, until a group of four lads decide to try and cause trouble. They start shouting about the slow service and I can feel my anger rising. They just so happen to be at my end of the bar as well. Bloody typical. I listen to their taunts for another five minutes, and then I decide that I have had enough. I march over to them and look at each of them in turn. They must only be eighteen, and they clearly can't handle their drink. I politely ask them to calm down or they will be removed from the premises. It appears though that my words have no effect on them. If anything, it seems to spur them on to act like even bigger assholes. One of the lads decides to try and act like a hero and lets himself behind the bar. He starts trying to pull his own pint and I look to see if security has noticed. They haven't. Looks like it's going to be up to me to do something for the time being.

"What the hell do you think you are doing?" I ask the young lad.

"Getting myself a fucking drink." He is slurring and has obviously had far too much alcohol already.

"Get back on the other side of the bar, now," I say in a slightly raised voice.

"What, so you can make us wait even longer? No chance love." That's it. I've had enough. I grab the pint glass out of his hand and throw, what drink that he has managed to pour, all over him. "HEY!! Why the fuck did you do that?" he asks, looking a little shocked. His mates are all laughing in the background.

"Get out from behind my bar, NOW," I shout. I hear Susie radio through to security, who still haven't noticed, and within seconds the young lad is removed from the bar. "Take his friends too," I tell security. They march the group of lads out and I continue to serve the other customers. Some of the customers waiting, who were near the group of guys, start to clap. I am shaking from the adrenaline rush of confronting the pissed up youngster. *Who the hell do some of these guys think that they are?* I don't have much time to reflect on it though, as it is just too busy. The rest of my shift flies by, but thankfully, goes more smoothly. Susie and I don't get a chance to take a break, so by the time we finish, at eleven thirty, we are both knackered.

"I'm sorry it was just the two of us tonight Susie." I feel bad that I couldn't manage to get anyone else to come in to help.

"No worries. It's all over now. Although, I am glad that I'm not in tomorrow. I am exhausted."

"Yeah, me too." We walk out of The Den and I see Jake's limo parked right out the front. I give Susie a hug good bye and tell her to enjoy her day off tomorrow. Eric is standing by the limo, with the door open for me.

"Miss Stacey," he nods as I get into the car. I just wave at him as I am too tired to speak. I sit down and squeal as I see that Jake is sat on the opposite side to me.

"Jeez Jake, you nearly gave me a heart attack," I say to him. His face does not look pleased.

"So, are we going to talk about earlier?" Jake gets straight to the point.

"Jake, I'm really tired and there is nothing more I can say to you," I sigh.

"I don't think that you are taking this situation with Caitlin seriously."

"Oh I am," I snap. "I just don't see why I should have to be cooped up when you're the one who fucked her and made her paranoid." I am tired, and what I have just said has come out wrong. I didn't mean to sound so harsh.

"So, that's how you really feel, huh? You think that I made her crazy?" Jake's eyes pierce into mine.

"No. I didn't mean it like that. I just mean that I am not staying under lock and key because of her. I can handle her Jake. I managed to survive the last run in with her. I don't want to live in fear." I try to reason with him, but it doesn't seem to be working.

"I don't want you under lock and key Stacey, I just want you safe, and until she has been dealt with, you are not. You are at risk."

"She wants you Jake, not me."

"Exactly. She wants me and she will do whatever it takes to get me. The quickest way to get to me, is to eliminate you." I can't quite process what he is telling me. It all sounds like too much. *Eliminate me?* I can feel a headache coming on and all I want to do is go home to bed.

"Jake, can we discuss this tomorrow? Talking about this subject when I'm tired really isn't the best time." I lay my head back against the seat and close my eyes.

"If you would just come and stay with me, then I wouldn't need to worry about you quite so much." I open my eyes and look at him. He is looking out of the window. I ease myself off of the seat and go and sit in his lap. I place my hand on his face and turn his head so that he is looking at me.

"Jake, I know that this must be difficult for you. I know that she is trying to hound every aspect of your life, but I can't come and stay with you. We have only just begun to see each other seriously, and look what happened the last time that I stayed at yours." Jake goes to speak, but I silence him by placing my finger over his mouth. "Even if that wasn't enough of a reason, I need to be there for Lydia right now. She's having a hard time at the moment and I need to stay with her." My finger is still on his mouth. He opens his mouth and sucks my finger, all the while looking into my eyes. My body shudders as I feel my sexual awareness heighten. I pull my finger out and place my lips on his. I kiss him softly, and run my hands through his hair. His hands are wrapped around my waist. We are locked together like this until we pull to a stop outside the flat.

"I just............... I don't want anything to happen to you," Jake whispers to me, breaking our kiss. I lean my forehead against his.

"Nothing is going to happen to me. I would invite you in to stay, but I don't think that Lydia needs to see a happy couple right now. I will call you tomorrow morning."

"You better, the minute you wake up." I giggle as Jake nibbles my ear lobe. I slowly move myself off of him as the limo door opens, meaning that Eric is stood waiting. I step out of the limo and Jake follows me. "I'm walking you to your front door."

"Don't be ridiculous. I will be fine."

"I'm walking you to the door, end of." I roll my eyes at him and say good bye to Eric as we walk to the flat. We reach the front door and I turn to give Jake a hug. He squeezes me and kisses my forehead. "What's wrong with Lydia anyway?" he enquires.

"Women's troubles." I am not telling Jake anything. Paul doesn't even know what has happened, and I don't want him to find out from Jake.

"Say no more," Jake says. He releases me and I unlock the front door. A thought suddenly occurs to me and I turn back around so that I am facing Jake.

"How did you know that I had gone to the shop earlier?" I ask. I am interested to know the answer.

"Eric was driving in the neighbourhood and he saw you."

"And why was Eric in the neighbourhood?" I think that I already know the answer but I would like to hear what response he is going to give.

"He was just passing through." Jake shrugs his shoulders.

"Uh huh." I know that Eric wasn't just merely 'passing through,' but I don't want to argue about it tonight. I will tackle the subject another time. "Goodnight handsome."

"Night babe." He stays where he is until I have closed the front door. I really wish that he could have stayed here. I could do with releasing some sexual tension. I sigh. *Never mind, there is always tomorrow.*

Chapter Thirty-Five.

I wake up at ten o clock the following morning. I stretch out in bed, before grabbing my phone off of the bedside table. I have one text message from Martin.

Hey girlfriend! I haven't seen you in forever!

Let's hook up for coffee ASAP! Much love,

Martin xxx.

I love Martin. He's an awesome person with such an infectious nature. I quickly text back that I can meet him in an hour at Danish. I feel really bad that I have neglected mine and Martin's friendship for a while. Martin is easy going, so I am hoping that he will understand why my mind has been so preoccupied, once I fill him in on all the details of what's been going on. I go and check on Lydia before I get dressed. She is asleep in bed so I don't disturb her. I heard her crying at some point during the night, so I figure that she must be exhausted. I go back to my bedroom, put some clothes on, and I leave a note for Lydia on the kitchen table. I let her know where I am going, and if she needs me to come back, then I have my phone with me. I put my essentials in my handbag, and I leave the flat. I decide to phone Jake on my way to meet Martin. He answers after a couple of rings.

"Good morning gorgeous," he says. His voice is so sexy.

"Morning handsome." My face breaks out into a smile and I can feel a slight blush creeping across my cheeks. "How are you on this fine morning?"

"I'm great. You?"

"I'm fantastic. I'm just letting you know that I am on my way to meet a friend for coffee."

"You're what?" his voice rises a couple of notches. "Please tell me that you called Eric and asked him to take you?" I can hear the strain in his voice and I feel a little bad that I am making him worry like this.

"Uh……… no."

"Stacey! Why do you not listen to me?" Frustration creeps into his tone and I imagine him sat at his desk, well a desk seeing as I have no clue what his personal office actually looks like, rubbing his temples to try to sooth some stress.

"Jake, calm down." I need to get him to understand that I need normality in my life. I don't want to abide by Caitlin's crazy rules. "I am talking to you on the phone, and I will be at the coffee shop in two minutes. Please don't be mad at me. I don't want to argue with you," I say. I hear Jake let out a sigh. "I will make it up to you later."

"Oh yeah? And just how are you going to do that?" he enquires.

"You'll see. I would divulge the details but I wouldn't want you getting all hot and bothered whilst you are at work." I love teasing him. "I've got to go babe, I'm at the coffee shop and my friend is waiting. Talk to you later."

"Okay. But, promise me that you will call Eric the minute that you need to go home," he insists. I choose to appease him on this matter, seeing as he has probably, very nearly, had a heart attack at me walking on my own for a few minutes already.

"Yes, I will call Eric. Bye handsome." I hang up the phone and am enveloped in Martin's arms.

"Baby girl, it's so good to see you," Martin says as he squeezes me tight.

"You too stranger."

"And whose fault is that?" Martin releases me and raises his eyebrows at me.

"Okay, okay. I've been a bad friend, but just you wait until you hear why."

"I'm all ears baby doll. Why are we still standing out here? Let's get inside, get some coffee, and get gossiping." I laugh and lead the way into Danish. My usual table is free, so we sit there and then order some drinks. It is nice and quiet in here, and there is no sign of a certain blonde haired psycho. I relax and start to tell an excited Martin all about my life over the last couple of weeks. It takes me a couple of hours to tell him everything. We get through three coffee's and a couple of calorie induced slices of cake. I don't hear anything from Lydia, so I assume that she must still be resting. I don't text her as I don't want to disturb her when she needs her sleep. I don't tell

Martin about Lydia. It's not my place to tell anyone about what she is going through. When Martin is satisfied that he has been updated sufficiently on my life, we leave Danish, and head to the nearest clothes shop. I need to purchase some sexy office attire, in order to surprise Jake. Martin helps me find exactly what I need and makes me try it on, so that he can see the full effect.

"Hot damn girl, he is going to be blown away when he sees you in this get up. Hell, if I were straight, I would do you." I giggle and smack Martin, playfully, on the arm.

"You're terrible."

"I just tell it like it is." Martin is always straight to the point and I love that about him. I get changed back into my original clothes, and go to pay for the items that I am purchasing. When we exit the shop, I call Eric and ask him to collect me. I have sneakily called Jake's office to make sure that he has a free appointment this afternoon. Luckily for me, he did. I then secured an appointment with him, under the name of Miss Green. I only have a thirty-minute slot as Jake has other meetings to attend. I am hoping that my visit to his office will be very memorable for the both of us. Eric pulls up outside the clothes shop a few minutes after I have called him. Jake must have given him a clue as to where I was for him to arrive this quickly.

"Well, this is my ride," I say to Martin as I point at the limo. His jaw drops open.

"You are so taking me in that one day," Martin says. I laugh and give him a hug goodbye.

"I promise I won't leave it so long for us to catch up next time."

"You better not." Martin winks at me and I disappear into the limo.

"Hi Eric," I say as I sit back in the seat.

"Miss Stacey," Eric nods. "Back to your flat?" he asks me.

"Actually, no. I need you to take me to Jake's offices, but it has to be a secret. I have a little surprise for him." I put on as much charm as possible and I see Eric smirking in the rear-view mirror.

"What the surprise?" Eric asks.

"Ummmmmm........." I feel my cheeks go red. I don't want to divulge my plans to Eric. I avoid eye contact with him and start to squirm in my seat, when Eric starts to laugh.

"It's okay Miss Stacey. From the look on your face, I'm guessing that whatever you are planning is for Jake and Jake only."

"Exactly," I reply. "Do you mind if I put the partition up? I.... I need to get changed." I feel embarrassed at having to ask.

"Sure." As I press the button for the partition to close, I see that Eric is still smiling. I feel a little uncomfortable that I have to get changed with Eric driving, but the partition is completely blacked out, so there is no chance that he will see anything. I don't think he would look anyway to be honest. He seems like an old-fashioned gentleman, and I get the impression that he is just happy to see Jake happy. Or, that's what I like to think anyway. I quickly pull the clothes that I have bought out of the shopping bags, and I start to get changed. I have to say though that putting on a skin-tight pencil skirt, in a car, is quite challenging. The skirt has a slit up the back, which stops just below my ass. I put on stockings and suspenders and a tight fitting white shirt. I finish the look off with a tight blazer, red lipstick, and I put my hair up into a high ponytail. As I am putting on the black stilettos that I purchased, we pull up outside Jake's offices. I quickly put on the long coat, that I bought, in order to hide my outfit from anyone else's eyes. I would be mortified if anyone other than Jake got a look at my outfit. Eric opens the limo door for me and I thank him. I go to pick up the bags with my original clothes in, but Eric stops me.

"It's okay Miss Stacey. You can leave that in here."

"Oh, okay. Thank you." I smile and give Eric a wave as I head inside the office building. Walking through the lobby, I get a few appreciative looks off of some men, but I ignore them and walk to the lifts. I select the relevant floor for Jake's office and am relieved that I am alone in the lift to go over my plan. The doors ping open moments later and I step out. To the left is a desk, with an older lady sat behind it. She looks up at me and smiles. She introduces herself as Valerie and asks me if she can help. I inform her that I have an appointment under the name of Miss Green, which she checks on her computer. She then gestures for me to take a seat in the waiting area, which is a cosy collection of plush chairs just outside of Jake's office. I hear her telephone through to Jake, and then she is telling me to go on through. I nod, take a deep breath, and I walk to the doors of his office. I open the doors and walk in. Jake doesn't look up, so I close the door behind me and lock it. His head snaps up at the sound of the lock.

"Good afternoon Mr Waters," I say, putting on the sexiest voice that I possibly can. My hands start to undo the long coat that I am wearing, and Jake's eyes go wide as I let the coat drop to the floor. I walk forward, slowly, until I reach the front of his desk. I want to laugh at the fact that his mouth has dropped open slightly, but I manage to suppress it. He, eventually, clears his throat and manages to speak.

"Please take a seat Miss *Green*." He motions for me to sit in the chair which is just behind me.

"Why thank you." I sit down, cross my legs and provocatively sit back in the chair. Jake smirks.

"Would you like a drink?"

"I don't have time for a drink I'm afraid. I am a very busy woman and I have other things that I need to attend to."

"Is that so?" he raises one eyebrow at me.

"It is indeed. So, shall I get to the point of why I asked for this meeting?"

"Please do," Jake says, never taking his eyes off of mine. He then sits back in his chair and awaits my answer.

"Well, I was hoping that you would provide me with a service that is going to satisfy my needs," I purr at him. Where this inner vixen is coming from, I have no idea, but it is doing exactly what I want it to. Jake's eyes look hungry. Hungry for me. I resist the urge to do a little jig in excitement.

"I'm sure that we could come to some sort of arrangement. What did you have in mind?" Jake asks, licking his lips. I slowly stand up and walk over to a sofa that is to the right of his desk. The sofa is plush, as is everything else that Jake owns.

"I think that we should get a bit more comfortable over here, don't you?" I say as I sit down and pat the sofa next to me. Jake stands and starts to stalk his way over to me. My heart does a little flutter at the mere sight of him. His stance is dominating, and it is such a turn on. I take off my blazer and throw it on the floor. My hands then start to undo the buttons on my shirt. I let out a small moan as Jake gets closer. I bite my lip in anticipation of his hands touching me. Jake takes off his suit jacket and then, before I know what is happening, he pounces on me. I squeal in delight and relish the feel of his hard body on top of mine. His lips devour me, and I run my hands through his hair. Jake kisses me passionately, and it is as if no one else exists. Jake pulls back from me slightly as we both try to catch our breath.

"I must say Miss Green, I think this meeting is going extremely well." I don't get a chance to answer as Jake's lips find mine again. Who knew that a bit of role play could be so much fun?

Chapter Thirty-Six.

The next few days pass by in a blur, and before I know it, it is Saturday. I have spent most of my time covering shifts for Lydia as she is still not in a good way. I have told her to speak to Paul, but she just says that she can't do it. She seems to think that avoiding him is the best answer. All I can do is be there for her and support her as best as I can. Working the extra hours hasn't been too bad, seeing as Jake had to out of town to attend to some urgent business two days ago. I have missed seeing him, but he is due back tomorrow evening and I can't wait. I have spoken to him on the phone, but it's not the same as having him here in person. I miss everything about him. His touch, his smell, his eyes, his laugh. I find myself daydreaming about him at every spare moment that I get. Things have progressed between us so quickly, in such a short amount of time. Every fibre of my being craves him. I know that I am in love with Jake. I haven't told him so yet as I don't want to get ahead of myself, but I do. If things don't work out with us, I know that I am going to be left heartbroken. Before Jake left, he made me promise that I would call Eric if I needed to go anywhere. I don't like bothering Eric, but I also need to keep Jake from worrying about me whilst he is away. The sooner Caitlin leaves us alone, the better. I haven't seen any trace of her for a few days now. Maybe she has finally seen that she isn't going to get her own way? I am sure that some other woman would have run a mile when Caitlin threatened them, but not me. I don't see why she should be able to dictate who Jake has in his life. And she sure as hell doesn't get a say in who I choose to be with.

My shift at The Den tonight starts at five o clock. I am starting earlier than normal due to needing to do some of Lydia's paperwork for her. It's a good job that not much has changed since I worked at The Den the first time, meaning that I understand what paperwork needs to be filled in and filed etc. I make myself a cup of coffee and also make one for Lydia. I take it through to her bedroom and leave it on the bedside table for her. She is asleep, which is all that she seems to be doing lately. I quietly leave the room, go back to the kitchen to get my coffee, and then I set up camp in the lounge with my laptop. I have the urge to do some more writing. I just want to finish the first draft so that I can then start editing my novel. I am so pleased with what I have written so far. I settle down and begin to type. The day flies by as I do nothing but type and drink coffee. Lydia doesn't emerge from her room at all. Nothing distracts me all day, and by four o clock I have to force myself to stop writing, save my work, and turn off my laptop so that I can get ready for work. I put my laptop back in my bedroom and then go and take a quick shower. I have forty-five minutes until Eric will be here to pick me up. I dry myself and dress in my usual skinny jeans, which I team with a black vest top, black cardigan, and black sandals. I have come to realise that flats are the best type of shoes to wear for work, especially with all the extra hours that I have been doing. Plus, there is less risk of me falling on my ass whilst carrying a tray of glasses. I tie my hair back into a loose ponytail, I apply some mascara and lip gloss, and then I am ready to go. Lydia still hasn't come out of her room, so I poke my head around the door to see if she is still asleep.

She's awake, but is just staring blankly at the television in the corner of her room.

"I'm going to work now Lyd," I say. Lydia just waves her hand at me, not even moving her head to look at me. I close the door and let out a soft sigh. I need to get her out of this funk that she is in. I also need to get her to leave the flat before she develops some kind of cabin fever. I hate seeing her so upset, even if it is for something that she has brought on herself. I grab my keys and handbag and head out of the front door. Eric is waiting outside for me, just as I knew that he would be. It has to be said that Eric is extremely punctual. I wouldn't be surprised if he had been waiting here for a while beforehand.

"Good evening Eric," I smile at him in greeting.

"Miss Stacey." His usual greeting to me is paired with a nod of his head. I enter the limo and sink into the luxurious seats for the short ride to The Den. I am the first one to arrive as the rest of the staff won't be in until six. We would normally be open all day today, but due to staff shortages, I had to put a sign up saying that we were closed for a couple of hours this afternoon. I could have used agency staff, but they aren't that great and there wouldn't have been any regular staff to come in and do the shift with them. I hope that I made the right choice. Eric says that he will be waiting for me when my shift finishes, at two in the morning, as I exit the limo. I politely thank him and unlock the front door of The Den so that I can go inside. I lock the door behind me as I will be in the office, and I won't be able to hear if anyone comes in. Plus, I don't fancy the idea of random customers coming in here when I am on my own. I pour myself a glass of diet coke and walk into Lydia's office so that I can get started. It takes me half an hour to go over the rota for the following week. I pencil Lydia in, but I have managed to sort the shifts so that, if she is still unable to work, then I can fill in whilst also leaving myself a break in between shifts. I print off the rota and stick it onto the staff notice board which is just by Lydia's office door. As I am tidying up the desk, there is a knock on the office door. I freeze. My mind races as to who could be knocking on the door. Also, more importantly, it has to be someone else who has a set of keys. *Who the hell could it be?* I stand, looking at the door, trying to decide what to do. I become fidgety and very aware that I could be in danger. *Shit, what should I do?* I grab my phone and type out a quick message to Lydia.

Lyd, just remind me, does anyone else

have keys to The Den? xx

I get a short reply back a few seconds later.

Only the owner, but he never comes down.

Why? xxx

I fire off a quick reply telling her not to worry as I try to calm my nerves. *Maybe it is the owner? But if it is, then why would he knock on the door?* Whoever is on the other side knocks again, making me jump. I need to remain calm.

Everything is going to be fine. I slowly walk over to the door and place my hand on the door handle. It feels like my heart is going to burst out of my chest. I close my eyes and take a couple of deep breaths. I open my eyes at the same time as I open the door, and the sight before me is not one that I am pleased to see. It's Caitlin. *Fuck! What is she doing here? More importantly, how did she get in here in the first place?* I stand as confidently as I can and straighten my back. Her eyes glare at me, but I will not look away. I am a strong woman and I need to show her that I mean business. She looks awful. Her blonde hair is all in disarray, and her eyes look wild. She is dressed in jogging bottoms, a t-shirt and trainers. It's almost as if she has given up on taking care of herself. *I wonder if she is high?*

"What are you doing here Caitlin?" I sound a hell of a lot more confident than I feel.

"I thought that we should have another little chat." She walks towards me and brushes me out of the way so that she can enter the office. I stumble slightly, but I soon regain my balance. I am a little taken aback by her brazen manner, but I shouldn't be. She has so far proved that she doesn't care how her actions are perceived. She takes a seat on the small sofa and crosses her legs. She really does think that she is something special. I would love to give her a slap and wipe that evil grin off of her face. I make myself move, and I sit on Lydia's office chair, behind her desk. I need to act as casual as possible, so I lean back in the chair and wait to see how this scenario is going to play out.

When a few minutes' pass by, and Caitlin still hasn't said anything, I decide to get the ball rolling.

"So, what is it that we need to talk about Caitlin? And you had better make it quick as I have staff arriving soon."

"Well, considering what I said to you, the last time that we spoke, has had no influence on your decisions whatsoever, I thought that I should make my intentions much clearer." She leans forward, but keeps her legs crossed.

"What do you mean by that?" I ask her, urging her to get to the point. I want to get her out of here as quickly as possible.

"When I told you to stay away from Jake, I thought that I had made myself clear, but it turns out that I didn't do a very good job of showing how serious I was about it. So, I am here to reiterate that message." I can't help but roll my eyes at her.

"Listen Caitlin, I have had enough of this. I understood you perfectly the last time, I just chose to ignore your empty threat. You have absolutely no right to dictate what Jake and I do. You two are finished. You really need to accept that in order to move on with your life." She doesn't move a muscle. "I understand that he hurt you and that he is sorry that he ever did that. I can't begin to imagine what you are going through. I am not a horrible person Caitlin, and I do have compassion for you, but the time has come for you to take a good look at yourself. You need to move on Caitlin and start living your life." I sound so calm and collected. I mentally clap for myself as I realise that I could be handling this situation completely differently.

"You don't understand anything," Caitlin screams at me. "You have no idea what Jake and I have been through. You don't understand anything. *You* are the reason that we aren't together, which means that I need to remove you from this situation." *Fuck, calm Stacey is no more. Remove? What is she talking about?* My heart starts to pump faster and I can feel adrenaline surge through me.

"What do you mean by, I need to be removed?" I manage to keep my voice steady as I speak. Caitlin's lips turn up into a smirk, and she lowers her eyes. I follow where she has lowered her eyes to. Her hand reaches inside the pocket of her jogging bottoms, and she pulls out a knife. *Holy shit! I need to get the hell out of here!* "Caitlin, what the fuck are you doing with that?" I ask, as I point a shaky finger to the knife that is clutched in her hand.

"I thought that this may be a little bit more persuasive than just words." I lower my hand and try to rack my brains for a way to diffuse this situation. I pray to God that the bar staff show up early. "It certainly seems to be having the desired effect." Caitlin gets up off of the sofa and stalks towards the desk. I push myself back, on the chair, until I hit the wall. I don't move that far back as the office isn't very big. Caitlin stands in front of the desk so there is still a barrier between us. Oh god, I need to keep her talking. Just until someone else arrives, and then I can alert them to what is happening.

"Caitlin, I think you need to put the knife away. We can just talk about things. I will listen this time. Just put the knife away before things get out of hand," I say in a shaky voice. I can no longer hide my fear from her. She is a crazy bitch and I curse myself silently for getting involved in the issues that she has with Jake. She doesn't move. She just stands there, with the knife in front of her, and her eyes are glaring at me. "Caitlin……. please? You need to think this through."

"Oh, I have thought it through. I have thought about how nothing would satisfy me more than ruining that pretty little face of yours." I gulp loudly at Caitlin's words. "Maybe if you didn't look like that, then Jake would come back to me." I can feel myself start to sweat. I look to the door and then back at Caitlin. I can't get out of here unless I run right past her. *Fuck, fuck, fuck!* I try to calm my breathing. I can feel the blood pounding in my ears. I can't even phone anybody because, like an idiot, I left my phone on the bloody desk when Caitlin got up and walked over. If I try to grab it, she will be able to reach me. Before I have time to think about anything else, Caitlin lunges over the desk. I let out a loud shriek and I force my legs to make me move from the chair. Caitlin has obviously misjudged my position as she lands on the floor just to the left of my chair. As she makes contact with the floor, I run. If the situation wasn't so scary, I think that I would be laughing at her attempt to lunge over the desk. As she is sprawled on the floor, I realise that this is my chance. This is my chance to escape. I run around the desk as fast as I can and I head for the door. I just think that I am about to make it safely out of the door, when Caitlin grabs my foot.

I yell and fall to the ground, smacking my head on the floor in the process. I block out the pain from hitting my head and I furiously kick at Caitlin. She manages to dodge each kick, but I don't stop. She still has a knife in her hand, and there is a chance that I will kick her and put a stop to her psychotic plan. I don't want to know what the end game is, but I have a fairly good idea of what she may have thought to do. I need to get away from her. I need to get her off of me. I try to struggle but she still has a vice like grip on my foot. I am screaming to alert anybody of my whereabouts. *Why has no one else arrived here yet? Surely someone should be here by now?* As I try to scramble away, I hear Caitlin let out an evil cackle. I feel her release my foot and I am about to get up, when I feel a sharp, piercing pain in my side. *Ouch, that fucking hurts.* I continue to scream as tears spring to my eyes. I can still hear Caitlin laughing in the background. Things start to go hazy and I stop screaming. I don't have the energy to keep screaming. I groggily lift my head and I look down my body to see the knife stuck in my side. Caitlin's hand is clasped firmly around the handle. My eyes shift to Caitlin, and all I see is her laughing like a deranged psycho. It feels like I am led here for hours, but in reality, it must only be a few seconds. Time has seemed to slow down in my foggy state. Images start to flicker through my mind as I start to lose consciousness. I hear footsteps and see two figures have entered the room. They are soon lifting Caitlin off of me. *Maybe I am hallucinating?* I don't take any notice of who the figures are until I hear one of them shout.

"NOOOOOOOOOOO." It's Jake. It's his voice. I try my hardest to speak to him, but I can't. My mouth won't work. I can feel myself losing the fight to stay awake. The darkness is calling to me, and it seems so inviting. My eyes are fluttering as I feel myself being pulled into someone's arms. I try to open my eyelids, but it's no good. I am far too sleepy. The darkness looks too good to resist. As I give into the urge to go to sleep, I hear Jake speak.

"Stacey baby, open your eyes. Please." I can hear him pleading with me, but no matter how hard I try, I can't open my eyes. I can still hear Caitlin's laugh echoing in the distance, and I want nothing more than for that noise to disappear. As her laughing eventually fades away, I hear Jake speak one last time.

"I love you," are the last words that I hear, before the darkness engulfs me.

THE END.

To continue reading Stacey and Jake's story, then read the second book in the Perfect Series. The second book is called Perfect Memories. Will Stacey survive? There is only one way to find out.......

I would like to thank my partner James for his patience whilst I have been working on my book series.

I would like to thank my friends who have listened to me talking about this for the last four years.

I would also like to give a special mention to my friend, cover designer and PR Guru, Vikki. You have been amazing and without your help I wouldn't have been able to do this.

I would also like to thank my readers. I hope that you enjoyed reading about Stacey and Jake as much as I enjoyed writing about them.

My final thank you goes to my children who I hope, one day, will be proud of me for achieving success as an author. I love you both very much.

©Lindsey Powell 2017

Printed in Great Britain
by Amazon